Destiny: When Your Soulmate Finds You

Rowan Knight

Published by 22 Lions Bookstore, 2017.

Table of Contents

Title Page

Destiny: When Your Soulmate Finds You
By Rowan Knight

Published by 22 Lions Bookstore and Publishing House

About the Publisher

About the 22 Lions Bookstore:
www.22Lions.com
Facebook.com/22Lions
Twitter.com/22lionsbookshop
Instagram.com/22lionsbookshop
Pinterest.com/22lionsbookshop

Dedication Page

This book is dedicated to the main protagonist of the story presented here. She insisted in wanting me to write a book about our relationship, but probably didn't realize that she was asking me as well to write a reality-based story, and not a fairytale or a fiction novel. And so I wrote the whole truth here, from when I fell in love with her up until what happened later between us, as well as what I know about her future. As a matter of fact, I added many of our conversations, exactly as we spoke to one another. And in the love of such truth, I want to thank her for giving me a whole meaningful experience, which will hopefully enlighten and motivate many others to seek happiness beyond the turbulences of insanity and disrespect that I have found myself experiencing. I hoped and still do, that one day she can read this book again and again, until she can realize what I wished for her to see from the start. I am sure that with every reading anyone can discover a new and deeper layer towards why we were destined to find each other, for that was indeed written in the stars — we were and will always be soulmates.

Introduction

I never imagined that one day my own knowledge and empathy would imprison me in a path towards real love, towards finding the woman I could spend the rest of my life with, but apparently, this is what happened. By following a more spiritual and uplifting path in life, I ended up encountering the ultimate challenge, which is to accept this truth with an open heart, in the least expected place I ever considered, a small city in the baltic region, named Vilnius. That's where I would find her, the woman who captured my soul in a strong way through the most captivating eyes I've ever seen.

In this story, there is a path of self-discovery, but also the discovery of two soulmates, and only freewill could ever tell what each one would do with the experience of witnessing the confrontation of the similarities, fears and differences being mirrored at one another. Were we meant to live towards a common goal or simply hurt ourselves? Were we meant to be together forever or just experience love for a while? Was sex the best we could offer to one another, or was there much more beyond that? I guess one day we can look back at what happened and answer these questions with more clarity. I can't say it hasn't been, at the very least, very intense.

Destiny

On September 2014, I left China and moved to a small town in Viseu — Portugal. Coincidentally, Gloria arrived in Portugal in that same month, but in Lisbon. Then, on October of the same year, I moved to the south of Portugal — Algarve. Gloria went there with her friends too, in the same month and for a few weeks of holidays. Interestingly, I spent those months alone, and would be very happy to have found her. I did notice her, passing by with others, but fate had not placed us yet together. She was still just another stranger to me.

On January 2015, she started a relationship with Rui, from Cape Verde, and my former girlfriend, Fang, from China, reentered my life by surprise to restart the relationship with me. Because of her, I moved to the United Sates for a couple of months. But a phone call from one of my cousins, whom I did not see for many years, inviting me to his house, made me travel back to Portugal, this time in Lisbon, to meet with him.

I saw Gloria a couple of times, passing by with her new boyfriend, as she was still studying in that same city. Something in my heart burned when I found her holding hands with him, as if my soul was telling me that she should be holding hands with me instead. In truly many moments, we could have met and begin our relationship. We crossed paths too many times, and for a while, we were both single. But for some reason, that did not happen. And yet, since my childhood that I had been having dreams with her hometown. I knew where she was, although I did not know how to find her. I knew how her hometown looked like, but I did not know in which country it was yet. Likewise, she was feeling a deep impulse to travel to Portugal to find me.

After ending my relationship in 2016, I traveled to Denmark, and again, nearly found Gloria, because she went there as well, to visit her parents. After that, I visited her country, when she was back already, and single again, now working as a waitress. I saw her in a restaurant, but for some reason, we wouldn't yet talk to one another.

It is intriguing to notice how many times we crossed paths, even looked at each other, but kept losing one another from sight. We were certainly meant to be together from birth, even if she was born much later than me. That would have to occur. But up until then, we didn't know how to call each other by the first name.

I went back to Spain after those holidays, and asked a couple of friends, who know cartomancy, to see in the cards where I should go next. They indicated me Lithuania. And so, I moved there for good. They were right, for I finally met her in the exact same night I arrived.

Sadly, by then Gloria already had a huge collection of former boyfriends and one night stands behind her back, and having a serious relationship wasn't in her mind any longer. I guess she was trying to compensate for the love she couldn't find, and losing her capacity to love along the way. Her soul needed me but her heart couldn't wait. Was Gloria seeking for love with every man she slept with? Was she trying to find me by sleeping with as many men as she could? Or had she simply given up on loving someone?

Gloria was still young, only 22yo, but already drastically changed by her past experiences, and more interested in sex than love. It was difficult to get to know her without any sexual intention. She seemed to be only interest in men to sleep with and nothing more than that. I was barely able to have a normal conversation with her, even though I did feel a strong chemistry between us. This chemistry was felt from the distance at first, even before we started talking to one another. I couldn't take my eyes from her, despite our obvious age gap. In a way, I believe our age gap was actually the best guarantee that I could make her happy and change her life in a good direction. My life was already going well, I was traveling the world and going wherever I pleased, and only sought to find someone like her to help me enjoy it more, with less loneliness and more love.

DESTINY: WHEN YOUR SOULMATE FINDS YOU

I wish I could make Gloria see what I could see and lead her towards thousands of years of memories that cross my mind every time I look into her eyes. But that is not possible. Something in her heart says that I'm right and that she can trust me, but she can't deny her fears, emerging with such feelings, fears which increase in intensity as she empowers herself with the emotions that come from the bottom of her heart, emotions that I do know well, but for her still seem confusing. And how can I explain to someone that I know the past lives she doesn't, that I can see her soul in its full spectrum, her many former manifestations, and identify the reasons that brought her to me, even beyond her reasoning or momentary desires?

While Gloria believes that everything between us developed too fast, it's not really fast enough for me, not fast enough when the insights of many lives blend into one, and at present moment. Life is too short to be wasted, and an opportunity like this can't be neglected.

At every step of the way, she benefited from the gift of freewill, a gift inherited in every human soul, allowing us to make our own choices, and explore a multitude of universes and realities. And this is why life is simple and complex too, as well as complicated. The complexities emerge from the many options I could see around Gloria, none of which I wanted her to take. These options, I wished her not to see. Because, they were illusions, and not more than that. Those options, which could turn into complications, emerged from the dwellings of her soul, when contemplating them, when becoming mesmerized and astonished by them, when thinking she knows things that she does not truly know, when trusting her eyes and impulses, even while her soul screams "no". These are complications that, when observing Gloria, inside this labyrinth, I could see pulling and pushing her as a wild storm, which she doesn't know how to control, a storm using the weakness of her heart as its strength.

The reason why her heart is weak, is because she never truly loved anyone. The simplicity of all this is too simple for her to see. And I fear showing it to her, for I risk losing her in doing so. If I show her our future, she will challenge it with fears. If I show her my feelings, she will test them. If I offer her my trust, she will threaten it. If I show her, who her real self is, she will laugh, like a madwoman who has never seen what hides behind the veil of her self-deceptive personality, and thinks of herself as being sane. But everything that I just said can be resumed to Gloria's identity. When Gloria tells me that she doesn't know herself that well, she is describing, in her own words, everything I've mentioned here. But I do know her, I know myself, and I know us, and I can show her this paradox. But such insights bring me to another point, which is the reason why I met Gloria. She represents a very important step in my spiritual journey, either she chooses to be with me forever or not. And that I can't erase anymore. It is done. And it is as it was supposed to be, because I have put such path ahead of my desires, will and fears. And could I have done it otherwise? Not when I observe the alchemical transmutation that brought me to Gloria. And yet, despite everything I know, once again, I lay my weapons down, I put my shield and helmet on the ground, and move forward, towards the invisible and my strongest enemies, with only a heart filled with will. This heart will live beyond my physical death. My will finds itself in her, her nature, with all its storms, volcanos and light as well. And this will can remain until our final days in this lifetime and beyond. Or it can simply vanish in its fulfillment. Because I can't deny that I love her, and I won't love her less in the years to come, as this love remains the same since I saw her, and will remain in the future I envision, a future that although depending fundamentally on her will, won't ever diminish what I feel already. The only thing that will ever change, if such is the word we can use here, is the certainty of my feelings, as they guarantee the certainty of my vision. This vision, constantly pulling towards a future that I know already, makes me act towards her, not just as a person I recently met, but someone whom I know that will transform, change and manifest a new reality in the years to come, if such is her will, within the boundaries of her soul's freedom and the depth of my heart.

I honestly don't think Gloria has a choice, because her nature is self-destructive. To allow our love to fade away in order for her to explore any other alternative, would be like succumbing to death. Gloria met me to live through me and I already know that. I appeared in her life as her last chance, and she certainly prayed for it. I know,...

— "I am the one you prayed for before I appeared in your life."

— "No way!", Gloria answered, while staring at my eyes, stunned with perplexity.

— "Yes, I know, this is the truth; Nothing in our relationship is a surprise to me, and this is why I know how to make you happy. The only thing I can't do is make your own decisions or control them, or control you", I assured her.

The Emotional Storms

I knew, when I arrived in Spain, that I wasn't supposed to be there. I knew, when I ended a five years relationship, and even before that, that it was meant to end from the very start. I also knew, when doing past life regressions, that I wasn't solving my past as much as I was preparing myself for a future in which Gloria would be included, as if one thousand years back in time had to fit within the present. And yet, despite knowing all these things, I couldn't stop my anxieties, fears, worries and desires, all of which built up the storms of my own ignorance. The storms pulled me towards many women that were pulled away as fast as they fell in love with me. I met many beautiful women that were as much in love with me as I was with them, and I could see how we were pulled apart from one another, because, despite whatsoever I might have thought, we weren't meant to be together. I was supposed to meet Gloria from the start.

There are meanings much stronger to life than what any reason can comprehend. And in these meanings, I find the voice of God, to Whom I obey despite my unawareness regarding His intentions. As a matter of fact, I know now that what lasted for five years with my still very beloved Fang, could have lasted for another five or even fifty, if she had not been pulled away from me, as I knew she would. A man was moved towards her path, to distract her, deceive her, and finally pull her away from me. And I do not know exactly what will be her fate, even though I can assume the most obvious already, i.e., that she will fail again and for the rest of her life. I also knew that our end was meant to happen. I was meant to change her, help her, make her richer and then lose her, and she is meant to never find me again.

Maybe things could have been different, but with every encounter, every word exchanged and every experience, we build our future. Hate, differences and needs, are only tools of deception, which the soul finds when love cannot be assimilated. And although we can say that everyone can love in their own way, with their own predispositions, we can't say that the nature of love differentiates itself from person to person. Because, you see, the one who finds barriers in the color of my skin or the weaknesses of my character, is blind. And to the blind, love remains invisible, as a ghost that touches you, embraces you in need, but can never be seen or recognized, not more than a brief and smooth breeze. This said, I know now as before, that I was being prepared in many ways to find Gloria. I wouldn't believe so, if so much had not happened to me showing exactly that. And I do know that not everything is about us, but there is far more in us than there was in my own life, as unbelievable as it might sound. To fall in love with Gloria wasn't as much a willingness of my heart, or a match of my desires, as it was a recognition of what I was meant to see when the time was right.

When I arrived in Lithuania and went on a meeting to find my friends, I saw dozens of people altogether, and felt confused, for my eyes showed me many souls but my intuition showed me Gloria only. My feelings were dispersed but my consciousness was telling me that she was the one, although my mind was arguing that such wasn't making any sense. We barely spoke and I purposely lied to her about my country of origin, saying that I was Spanish. And yet, when she said in our first conversation that she loved Portugal, it was as if she was shouting at me again: I am the one.

I also don't know what was happening inside of her, because it seemed like my natural attitude of being cheerful and playful with everyone was creating a storm of thoughts and emotions inside of Gloria's mind and body. I saw her completely losing control over herself, and hysterically laughing at every joke I was making, as if her brain was spinning out of orbit. At one point, she started hitting me with her gloves and sarcastically telling others that I'm a psycho. But I believe that what really happened is that she had absolutely no idea of how to control herself, as I was taking that control away from her with all the emotions my presence was causing. The signs were hitting me from various angles, the emotions between us were obvious, and our connection was rapidly being built as well, beyond any logic anyone could perceive, but I still didn't feel safe in such belief. At the same time, I was actually afraid to make another mistake in my life. I did too many mistakes in the previous months, and didn't want to repeat them.

DESTINY: WHEN YOUR SOULMATE FINDS YOU

On the second night, everything became clear, at least, clear from one standpoint, because from another viewpoint, it was all getting more confusing within my mind. But maybe I had fallen in love before I knew I was already in love. Gloria came to me, punching my stomach with a crazy laugher in her face, and having fun in doing so, basically, screaming and bullying me around. There was no storm from which she would emerge as I was told, because she was the storm itself, and she didn't stop. I tried to stop her in any way I could, but Gloria was completely out of control. And then, when noticing I wasn't reacting, but actually confused by her behavior, Gloria decided to kiss my best female friend while smiling at me in defiance...

— "Are you jealous?", she asked.

Gloria was clearly pushing me to kiss her in any way she could. She even held my hands and grasped my ass, and in doing so, unveiled herself quite obviously. I had no more doubts but she was much younger than I expected and there was absolutely nothing in our conversations that could make me believe we have anything in common. Nothing was making any sense.

When I noticed that she felt rejected, unloved and unappreciated in her efforts to get me to kiss her, I did what seemed reasonable in my heart, which was to hug her and kiss her forehead. I was definitely feeling the same as she was, I also wanted to kiss her, but at that point, a hug seemed more reasonable to me. And yet, with every hug, I felt getting closer to her heart, while opening mine. I also had no idea why I was hurting her so much by rejecting her, but I wasn't ready to accept what was occurring between us.

I acted worse on the following day, by making jokes about it, and telling Gloria that she's too young for me, that I don't want her to act crazy around me anymore. And well, among a mix of truths with lies, I was also subliminally saying that I was falling in love with her but wasn't sure if she was in love too, or playing with my heart, or as much confused as I was. I didn't want my attitude towards her to be unilateral, I was unsure of her intentions, and I didn't know what to do about this situation. My next step was to push her towards Arthur and other guys, because, well, I wanted Gloria to do a mistake that would justify not seeing her again. That would eliminate all doubts I had. But she didn't do such mistake.

I saw her talking to other guys in the following nights we met with our group, and observed her from afar, waiting for a mistake to come, a mistake that would justify ignoring her. And while I waited, I was feeling jealous too. This jealousy didn't make any sense, because we were just friends, we barely knew each other, but I couldn't bare seeing her near any other guy, or talking alone with any guy. I was getting crazy. And I controlled this anxiety as much as I could, and within the need to see her jump into the arms of someone else. But she didn't do that, which made me more impatient. And so, I decided to invite her for a coffee, as I needed to know her better.

She refused, and showed no interest in talking to me anymore. Feeling rejected, she naturally ignored me, as if I had no value. I though I could play the same game but I couldn't. In the following night, when we went out with our friends, and I ignored her, I felt very depressed, and decided to go home earlier, because I couldn't bare it. And that's why afterwards, and despite the fact that she kept ignoring me, I put efforts to make her talk to me, or at least manifest some reaction. Sometimes I was happy to just see her angry. I would rather see her angry than having no reaction at all. When after my teasing moments she eventually punched my arm, I knew I had her. It was just a matter of time to correct my past mistakes and fix what I had broken. If love was there, it would certainly manifest again like a blossoming flower looking for its sun.

For reasons that surpass me and despite the fact that Gloria was ignoring my messages, I felt bad for letting her spend Valentine's Day on her own, but also had make sure I wasn't playing the fool by asking her out. I asked first if she had any plans for that night, and as she told me that she didn't, inviting her seemed natural. Somehow, I was behaving as if she was my girlfriend already, and feeling it too. But everything I had planned for that evening was a friendly dinner, and a rose as a gift. After all, it was the first time we were together, just the two of us.

I couldn't stop the emotions inside of me, and it was quite obvious that she was feeling the same. I though that one hour later Gloria would go back home, but she kept delaying catching the bus, hour after hour, as if willing to spend the whole night with me. At the same time, I could see that she enjoyed each moment in which I touched her hands, and often laid them at the table waiting for more. The chemistry between us was undoubtedly noticeable, and we quickly solved our past issues, and any resentment that could still be attached to our misunderstandings. After several hours of conversation, it seemed as if Gloria was waiting for something to happen between us, so I took the next step which was to lean towards her for a kiss. She refused. But I could see how happy she was to know I was falling for her. She then asked me to take her to the bus stop, and I wasn't sure if she was floating or jumping on the way, but she wasn't certainly walking. Her joy was too obvious to be hidden.

Due to a lack of any signal pointing at another direction, and for a few days, I though everything was over between us, and so I had given up. But then, when I met our friends again and Gloria was there, I could see how joyful she was for seeing me, not as before, but as someone that she wanted to continue playing with. She handed me a hidden message on a piece of paper, when nobody was watching: "Love is...".

It was quite obvious that she was requesting some more chasing on my part. She enjoyed being pursued and desired.

I didn't chase her because I wasn't sure of what to do anymore. I don't have patience for such games either. But when she asked to meet me in the morning of the following day, before her flight to Denmark, I knew she was enjoying my company, and I went with her to the airport to see more of this movie of hers, while noticing, on the way there, her curiosity about where I would be living, where I would rent my next apartment, and much more. It's as if she was introducing herself to my life, even though she had previously denied being part of it.

Gloria seemed afraid to be in a serious relationship, but the first thing she did on arrival and when meeting her family, was to text me, not once, but several times. I believe she was trying to keep my attention on her, making sure I wouldn't forget her. And it is because I could see this joy in her that I persisted and invited her out again when she returned to Lithuania.

We were holding hands too often, spending too many hours together, and when I walked her home, I felt myself getting insane with her need to avoid becoming serious about our relationship, just to force me to continue playing this game. Was she just interested in having sex or in continuing the romance? I ended the doubts by kissing her when she couldn't deny it.

Days later, and to my surprise, Gloria invited herself to sleep at my place. And since then, she remained in my life.

Disagreements & Implications

Thirteen days after our first date, we had our first breakup. I was hoping it would the first and last time we do such things to one another but I was wrong. It was a sign of what was about to come and repeatedly. I couldn't understand why Gloria arrived from work with so much anger and bitterness. I asked if it was my fault and she replied that it wasn't, and even apologized many times. However, she couldn't stop nagging about all kind of things the whole way, about my need to save money, my attire, and on and on, as if determined to push me away. And well, I lost patience at some point, and when she started nagging about that as well, it was the last drop. That's when I decided that maybe she's just not ready for a serious relationship, maybe she's not mature as a woman to be with me, and still has the brain of a child.

Adam: — "I don't have many more years to keep doing mistakes. I am looking for something serious and long term, and wasn't with you because of your attractiveness or sex. I was with you because I really like you. The main question is: who do I really like? If the Gloria I see or the one you see in yourself. Because, if when you look in the mirror, you see a resentful and angry person, a snake that needs to bite and poison, then you're not seeing the person I see, which is a joyful, funny, dedicated, caring, sweet and smart woman with a great sense of humor. I fell in love with the second image, not the first, and I don't see how testing my commitment, by being insulting, would do you any good. You won't prove anything with that behavior but merely push me away. But you're still young. You have many years to learn and do mistakes, and find someone who wants you."

Gloria: — "This is why I said I don't like when someone falls for me".

Adam: — "I love you Gloria", and I don't think it really matters who falls for who.

Gloria: — "You don't deserve to be with a person like me."

Adam: — "It's not about deserving. I can't stop what I feel for you from the beginning. You pushed me away today. And I do love your personality and qualities. I do enjoy spending time with you. If you want to spend the night with me, you can. I never said you couldn't. But you need to understand that you can hurt me. Wanting to be with you was a risk I was willing to take. But as I said before, and many times, you have freewill, including the freewill to push me away."

Gloria: — "I know. I don't hurt my friends. Never! I hurt the people who fall for me. And it has always been like that."

Adam: — "It doesn't have to be like that anymore."

Gloria: — "I cannot control myself."

Adam: — "Maybe you can let me help you do that, if you really want to be with me. Do you want to be with me tonight?"

Gloria: — "Yes, I do."

I still don't know if the reason for her behaviors came from the stress of her job, but whatsoever was the cause, if she kept testing and resisting the energy that brought us together, she would eventually be cutting the link that connected us. I think our first fight was the first test on her, and not me, to make her realize that we love each other, because, while in her mind the question was, "Is this love real?", destiny made her question something else instead: How far was she willing to go to either keep it or lose it?

Destiny only makes sense when people accept it, and doing so consists of taking into our hands the responsibility of making it happen according to our desires, of enjoying the path and not just flow with it. Relationships demand hard work and aren't based only on luck. But seems that Gloria has no self-control. On the following day, Gloria went back to the previous behavior, this time nagging about other issues, such as my tendency to forget things, the way I organize the house, and so on. And I still don't know why she keeps doing these things, but I can't make efforts on my own to keep the relationship going. Gloria told me that when she was younger, dreamed about marrying at 23yo. But would she want to be a wife that complains every day to her husband, smokes weed and gets drunk with her friends? I don't see in which way this makes sense. It has nothing to do with herself as a person. Such actions only match a self-image of what she built. Indeed, if she thinks that she doesn't deserve to be happy, get married and have her own family, then she is doing an excellent job to lose that chance from me because I was ready to take that boat with her. Respecting me would be a good starting point, as I can't share my life with someone who disrespects me.

This world is a big bubble of major mistakes but the story is always the same, as most people have low self-esteem, insecurities, and then think they can trash someone else to test their love, as if calling me names the whole day would make me feel like superman. Of course relationships don't work like that. I learned that the secret to a good relationship is in the heart, in accepting differences, and not the brain, not in trying to fix what doesn't work, as that means having a brain against brain competition. If there isn't mutual respect and mutual admiration, love is weak and doomed to fadeaway. I do want to get married, as I'm fed up of being single and dating girls like I'm inside a contest all the time, and I really like Gloria, but she's too young to show so many mental issues already. The key to make this relationship work is in the heart, in how much she can love me, because this is where things either follow through or break apart. We have to take chances in life. We only live once. It's better to crash and burn than never fly anywhere. And maybe nowadays most women are like this, insecure and insulting, as I see too much of it anyway, but that's not why I was with Gloria. I want to be happy and I believe she is a person that can bring me towards that happiness.

Gloria has good qualities, but I am equally happy in seeing her cooking in a shirt, sharing jokes with her, and simply spend time together. The problem is that Gloria has a tendency to be very selfish and I don't see how can she imagine a relationship like this, completely focused on her egotistical needs and wants. I truly believe in strong and faithful relationships, that uplift our heart and enrich our spirit, but they demand a constant overcoming of problems that will always emerge, with plenty of teamwork regarding keeping everything that make us happy beyond the relationship itself, namely, her friends, my friends, her activities and my activities, all in a perfect balance between differences and similarities. And the more joy we share, the faster I will propose her marriage, because, at that point, I can't imagine myself losing her to anyone else, living without her or living with anyone else. A relationship is a big investment of the heart and I'm willing to invest my heart on her. But that investment starts with accepting responsibilities, which, so far, I haven't been seeing in Gloria.

Every time she hurts me, I question myself if she's the wife I'm looking for, and every time this happens, I wonder and question about the real value of the best moments we spend together.

On the other hand, I learned from personal experience that you can't keep both options at the same time, you can't feed the thought of loving one person and losing it too. You can't feed the idea of ending the relationship and keeping it at the same time. The chances for success with absolutely anything in life tremendously increase when we burn the ships that brought us to a new land we must conquer. I have arrived at her heart and leaving isn't an option for me. In fact, I don't see any other option to be made here, because as soon as I decided that I wanted to be with her, the choice was made. I never doubt my decisions, simply because certainty tremendously increases the potential for success. The more certain I am about this, the easier it is to find ways to love her better. My ability to make Gloria happy in so many ways, with massages, jokes, sex and compliments, among other things, comes precisely from this rooted certainty. All my good and impressive actions are fruits of this tree called "making Gloria happy". But is she interested in making me happy or just receive happiness? I gave her the chance to choose:

— "There is a Native American tale about a story of two wolves. A grandfather is talking with his grandson and he says that there are two wolves inside each one of us which are always at war with each other. One of them is a good wolf, representing things like kindness, bravery and love. The other is a bad wolf, representing things like greed, hatred and fear. Then the grandson stops and thinks about it for a second; he then looks up at his grandfather and asks: "Grandfather, which one wins?" And the grandfather replies, "The one you feed". Gloria, you can choose to feed the love you feel for me or the fear of having a serious relationship. Either way, whichever you focus on, wins."

The Wolf You Feed

I have many memories that can't be erased, and the challenge now consists in evolving beyond them. It's possible to do that. I try to focus on the greatest surprises of life, the possibilities, emerging from the future. But this morning Gloria spent the whole way nagging as usual, and then looked back at me and asked...

— "Why are you so happy in the morning?"

— "Can you hear the birds?", I asked in return.

Gloria became silent, moving her eyes towards the ground as if embarrassed, and I continued...

— I don't need to wake up at 6AM like you do, I don't need to leave the house with you when you go to work. But when I look at your eyes, I don't really see any problem in doing such things. On the contrary, it's a pleasure, a pleasure added by small things that I take from the moment I open the door, such as the sunrise, the smell of fresh air, the singing of the birds, and much more. And surely enough, I wasn't always like this before, but everything can be learned, including the appreciation for life itself."

— "And why did you stopped meditating and doing your morning readings", she asked.

— "You want to know the truth? I did it because there's nothing more overwhelming to me than waking up with you by my side and massaging your head. I love to feel your golden hair curling between my fingers as I pass my hands softly by your head. I love to feel your back in my hands, when I cuddle you in the morning and at night before sleep. And I love to get lost, completely lost, and disappear in the colors of your eyes, that beautiful and magical blend of yellow with light green. Your eyes are like mandalas. And feeling hypnotized by the experience of looking at you is as spiritual to me as doing meditation.

Loving you is not just a feeling but a whole experience that uplifts my existence, including, and especially, when I'm challenged by your bitterness and anger towards the world. I just want to love you more in those moments. This is also the reason why this morning I decided to hide several messages in your belongings, telling you how much I appreciate having you in my life. I wanted to remind you during every moment of the day that you are important to me at many levels. When I met you, I knew that you had many hidden qualities, many attributes that weren't manifesting due to lack of awareness, and well, since we live together, you've never stopped impressing me in many ways. Apart from being beautiful, you know how to dress graciously, and you can be super creative as well within your own fashion style, alternating it constantly while always looking good. But this is far from being enough. Your abilities to cook are impressive. You cook better vegetarian food than what I ever ate in any vegetarian restaurant. And your attention to detail and beauty in a dish is admirable. Never before did I feel the urge to take photos of dishes until I saw yours. You are also truly caring in many ways."

Gloria was speechless. It is said that we never know how much we love someone until we put love to the test, and ours had been tested several times already. I thought I would lose her in every single one of those moments, and nonetheless, something inside of me was always saying that I should continue. And this reason, I must say, is the root of my confidence. It is for this reason that I didn't fear our disagreements, and also for this reason that I always found a way of speaking to her heart. And I wanted her to know this too...

— "I speak to you always and only with my heart. I see what my heart shows me that I must tell you. And you do have freewill to react as you wish, to listen or not to my words. But, you see, even though you may tell me that you never behaved with anyone else as you behave with me, what you do, your reactions, match what I know about us. To resist what we feel would mean to break something already built. We're not building a romantic story but living it. We have already wrote it before we were born. This is the reason why I told the Cherokee legend of the two wolves. I wanted you to know that you have the power to be happy, to choose happiness and keep happiness, without any fears. Whatsoever has occurred in your past, is part of it. And you should never start sentences by saying, "I am" but instead "I was". Who you are now is far greater than who you were, because you are blending with an emotion that is changing you in a very good way, the emotion of love. You have the power to feed either the wolf of ego, fear and anger, or the wolf of love, compassion and empathy. You shouldn't allow small misunderstandings to distract you from the main goal. When last Friday I refused to hold hands in public and show to others that we were together, as I wasn't ready for their reactions and judgments, it hurt your feelings, but I didn't want to lose you because of that, and that's why I said sorry. When you stopped to hear me, you listened, not necessarily to me, but my heart. You fed the wolf of love inside of you. And then we had a great weekend together, instead of spending it feeling resentment for one another. We both have a lot to learn but it has nothing to do with cultural differences, language barriers or even the age gap between us. Life experience and previous relationships have shown me that it doesn't matter if my companion is ten years older or ten years younger than me, or even of my own age. Maturity and behavior don't correspond to intellectual compatibility, cultural compatibility or even a similar background and dreams. The only thing that makes people compatible, as I know now, is love."

Gloria was overwhelmed with my words, but it was probably more than she needed to know. She interrupted me to give me a warning about her needs...

— "You're spoiling me by telling me every day that I am beautiful, that I have beautiful eyes and that you love my smile. One day you may forget to say it, and the stopping of the habit will make me resentful."

— "This won't ever happened. And how do I know? Because I'm not just appreciating you, but being thankful when I appreciate and admire you. You see, I don't just love you, but also love everything you represent to me. When I cuddle you, I'm practicing a daily ritual. When I make love to you, I'm practicing the religion of love. When I love you in your moments of bitterness, I'm practicing the art of love. When I speak to you, I'm verbalizing the best books of my life. When we hold hands outside, I'm practicing gratitude towards the world. When we smile together, I'm enjoying life entirely. I feel our love in every single moment, and I love that too."

When You Take Love For Granted

Nothing of what I say and do is enough for Gloria. Maybe she can't love. Because in just a couple of weeks, she seemed to have lost interest in keeping the relationship. Or did she took me for granted? Gloria didn't return home in the evening after work and I called her to know why:

Adam: — "Where are you?"

Gloria: — "In a bar."

Adam: — "Are you planning to come home?"

Gloria: — "I don't know. I didn't say anything because you complain about it. And you didn't talk in the morning, just ignored me, even if you were awake. But whatever, if you say that I have mental issues, but you chose to be with this kind of person, so who is stupider: me or you? You know, on social media people are nice, but in real life is shitty."

Adam: — "Gloria, you can't just go to a bar and laugh at my face. If you are coming home, you have to say it, and if you go to a bar after work, you have to say it too."

Gloria: — "We didn't talk the whole day. Why should I be obligated to say what I do after work?"

Adam: — "Because we are in a relationship and we live together, or are we not? It's almost 10PM. You can't just say nothing and then tell me, "I don't know if I'm going home". What is that? Are you coming here or planning to get drunk the whole night? Because I have a life too, you know."

Gloria: — "Calm down! I won't come back if you are on fire. Is it better if I won't come back today?"

I knew this was just the beginning of the abuse, so I said nothing. And half an hour later, Gloria replied:

Gloria: — "Ok, understood."

What Gloria did by ignoring me to go to a bar with friends and not sleep at home wouldn't be forgotten. The disrespect had crossed the boundaries of what I could tolerate,...

Adam: — "I reacted to the fact that you've been offending me every day, not talking to me, and disrespecting me by ignoring me when talking to others. Yesterday you did the same. If you don't think you have to apologize for the fact that I was waiting for you at home, then I'm very sorry you can't realize that, really sorry, because you see, I do love you, but you've been feeding the wrong emotions. I've done my best to make you happy. I don't deserve to be hurt. I do love you, but maybe you just don't know what that is."

Gloria: — "I got bored with you. For the things I ask, the answers are always the same: 'something simple, it's ok, it's up to you, we can do whatever you want'. I need to think for both of us. For me, it's not interesting like that. I am sorry if I offended you, but I didn't want to come back. You just ignored me in the morning. Whatever, it is what it is."

Adam: — "You spend the whole day at work and I only see you before work, when you sit in the bus without talking to me, and after work, when it is more important for me to be with you than what we eat or do. You don't have to think for both of us or think at all. You never did. Because I've even been the one cooking dinner for both of us. Besides, it's very hard to suggest things you keep rejecting. How can I make a decision for both, when the first five things coming out of my mouth are rejected? And I'm happy to know you don't like to be ignored, as it's a very good step towards understanding how you hurt others when ignoring them. And no, you cannot do whatever you want when you want, and step on me. The world doesn't move under your rules. And I feel very sad to realize that you saw me in such a superficial way. I only see you for three hours between your work and our sleep, and if you have gym, one hour. Most of the times, I'm next to you, alone, while you are playing with your mobile and texting to friends. You are the one with a boring life and ignoring me every day. Then, you project on me your anger and frustrations, as if it was my fault. You were the one destroying the relationship, because you don't feel comfortable with happiness and you don't respect me. That's why whatsoever I say, you criticize. I'm really sorry that you chose this path, rather than talking to me about it. I expected far much more from you."

Gloria: — "Well, it was a bad choice to choose a girl with mental issues and boring life."

Adam: — "Gloria, this is why I'm letting you go, as you were clearly not happy with me. I did a mistake when thinking that you were the person I could spend the rest of my life with. You're not wise enough to understand freewill or mature enough to comprehend love. And you did a mistake when thinking that I could smoke weed with you and get drunk with your friends. If that is the type of husband you dream about having, then maybe you should check dating.weed.lovers&alcoholics.com and see your options there."

Gloria: — "Thanks!"

Adam: — "And sorry for offending you, by calling you crazy, but your friends do that all the time, and I thought you liked it. 'I'm a mad woman', you say. I simply acknowledged it."

Gloria: — "Crazy, stupid, idiot or with mental issues; every word is different and has its own strength."

Adam: — "The meaning is the same. The difference is that your friends don't worry about how you feel at the end of the day. They'll just share beers with you. I didn't just welcome you into my house. I welcomed you into my life. I knew you were crazy from the start, and I insisted that you meet your friends, but not necessarily without letting me know as you did yesterday on purpose. I wanted you in my life because of the things your friends can't see in you, things that even you are still discovering in yourself. I didn't make this choice in one day. It took me a whole lot of time to understand what I was doing, and I couldn't have done it if you didn't want to be with me. But Gloria, if you never loved me, at least learn to love yourself. That was what I intended for you as well. I didn't force you to be with me. I just told you that I was in love with you and that it made sense for me to be with you. You don't need to hate me for loving you. I can do that without you too. I won't stop loving you even if we are apart. I was doing that already anyway."

The Push & Pull Game

Gloria felt me departing from her life for good and decided to pull me back in again with the fear of losing me. I allowed it, thinking that she understood her lessons, but our reconciliation wouldn't last long. Her friend Samantha invited her to go clubbing and Gloria couldn't resist, even if I was sick that day. Another fight started when she came back:

Adam: — "You abandoned me at home while I was sick to go party with your friends in another city and then sleep in the house of another guy. It shows the very opposite of what I did for you when you were sick, which was to stay with you the whole day, cook for you and take you to three different hospitals."

Gloria: — "Adam, I do love you and if I am with you, it means I dedicate myself to you. And if I had any doubts, I would tell you. I know you were cheated before, but I am not willing to do anything similar. I really do want to be with you. I want you in my life."

Adam: — "My goals and values are different from yours. We are not in the same boat. And I don't want to argue anymore about it."

Gloria: — "But we were in the same boat. We had the same goal."

Adam: — "We were never in the same boat. That is why we fight so much. You want a relationship, but not with someone like me. And the same applies to me. I think you saw me as an opportunity to travel and quit your job, but you don't really want to be under my wings, just receive the benefits of it."

Gloria: — "If you think like that, that I just want to benefit from you, this is an offense for me."

Adam: — "Since the beginning of the relationship, you asked for rings, cars, a house and even a smartphone, but you never committed to anything. You just looked at me like a walking ATM machine. You say that you are slow in falling in love, but you loved previous boyfriends much faster than you loved me. You also say you avoided me because you didn't know how to talk to me, but you did enjoy the company of other men in our group. You are ashamed to bring me to your friends and coworkers, and when faced with a decision, you set me apart, and you part without me. It is very clear to me, more than clear, that you don't love me and never did. I don't want to perpetuate this drama any longer. You get offended with the truth, but you are a slut and a gold digger. You never loved me. You used me."

Gloria: — "Apologies for that!"

Adam: — "Why do you apologize for things you do on purpose? You are happy being as you are, and you are happy with your life. The only problem was me. You don't know what is to truly love someone. Maybe one day you will know, and then you will know how you hurt me. You make me regret talking with you since I know you, because you are selfish and evil. You enjoy hurting people that like you. I thought that by being in a relationship you would change, but it just got worse. I do love you but I don't like anything in your behavior, and I am sure you need a psychologist if you ever want to have a normal relationship with me. You did not meet me to have another short night of sex with some stranger. But you cannot be in-between either. All the fights come from the fact that you don't want to make decisions, and you want to push me instead. But I know how this ends. You underestimate me a lot, you undervalue me a lot,... you don't really respect the person I am. But with every decision, the future is made. And you know what else Gloria, I don't like to be insulted with your ignorance anymore. If you are stupid, that's fine, but don't laugh at what I say because you don't understand it. Don't tell me any more that you don't need to see a psychologist. If you are happy with the person you've become, then what you feel for me means nothing to you. You insulted me a lot, and you keep doing it. But you made yourself vulgar and empty like that, and I am ready to move on without you."

Gloria: — "I do want to be with you."

Adam: — "My life, my goals and my values and rules are non-negotiable. As for your past and the things you did,... they made you who you are now. It's up to you, how much pride you have on that, and how much you want me to hate you by laughing at my face. I am not a target for the hate you have inside of you."

Gloria: — "I hurt you. You hurt me."

DESTINY: WHEN YOUR SOULMATE FINDS YOU

Adam: — "No! You insulted me in very evil ways and I reacted. It's like this for a long time."

Gloria: — "We both insulted and mistreated each other. Maybe it was a consequence of my own actions, but you set fear in me. I started to be afraid of you, which is not normal at all."

Adam: — "Yeah, I can see how much fear you have by your screams in the house. The day a man slaps you is when you know how fears feels."

Gloria: — "I do love you, but maybe not in the way you wanted, or maybe I just did not know how to."

Adam: — "Really? Do you know what love even is? Didn't you say that you only respect your friends? Then you love them, not me."

Gloria: — "I don't want to end in fights. You are the best I have ever met besides the negativity we had."

Adam: — "The negativity was brought by you, even before we started dating. You have been insulting me since I met you."

Gloria: — "I need your help."

Adam: — "I have helped you enough. You insulted me with what you learned from me. So why should I give you information? So that you can have more tools to insult me? You need therapy, not knowledge. Better a stupid psychopath than a smart one."

Gloria: — "I am really sorry if I disappointed you more than you deserve, more than you expected. I want all the best for you."

Adam: — "If you wanted the best for me, you wouldn't flirt with other men in clubs or insult me by saying, 'I do whatever I want'. Grow up!"

Gloria: — "I am sorry if I wasn't the one you always wanted in your life. That I made you believe in this. You believed in me, you believed in me more than I believe in myself, you see values in me that I have never seen in me, you found my qualities that I couldn't find..."

Adam: — "You never liked me. This chat is just more bullshit to victimize yourself. Didn't you say, 'You're too fucking old' and 'I don't love you'? Didn't you chat with former boyfriends after being with me and texted other guys from my own bed? So who the hell do you think will believe you now?"

Gloria: — "I don't feel satisfied with relationships after we go in opposite directions. After my last breakup I have promised myself to find better and not do such things. I promised myself to keep a relationship because to come over it is difficult, it hurts in all possible ways. But then I tell myself, if I got over once, I can do it again. It breaks my heart when you are in the same house, but not with me, not looking at my eyes, not talking to me, not seeing me at all. Sleeping in the same bed, but not hugging. It hurts me when you don't even believe what I say. You approve the answer you want to hear and ignore the rest. It makes me mad. So how can I tell the truth when you skip it? Of course, after that you call me a chronic liar... A happy marriage is about three things: memories of togetherness, forgiveness of past mistakes and a promise to never give up on each other"

Adam: — "There is nothing about me to forgive, but there are many things about you that can't be forgiven, ever. You are very smart when you answer what I write or say, but I can clearly see from which topics you runaway the most. You do use what you learn from me, but to keep the upper hand on your manipulation. Do not assume that I am so stupid not to see it. There is no memory of togetherness between us. I have no good memories with you. Why should I promise not to give up on someone that never committed to me? I have no idea why you insist in stalking my life. You are childish, immature and with severe mental traumas... But look, I am not your psychiatrist or psychologist... It's not my business to explain you all the mental diseases you have. The Adam you think you like, lives only in your head Gloria. The real Adam doesn't like you anymore and doesn't want to be with you. I don't want this drama anymore. And put this in your head: We don't have relationship fights or cultural differences. We have a grown up man putting up to an immature woman that is insulting, revengeful, immature, promiscuous, narcissistic, a liar, manipulative, selfish, irresponsible,... and all of these things for a whole year already. We don't have a marriage because we never had a relationship. You don't know what that is and you don't know who I am. You never loved me or respected me and you don't even know what both things are. I don't know why you are so obsessed with me, but you clearly never liked me. You have a poor sense of identity and that makes you very vulnerable to people who don't really want your best. You can't correlate your low self-esteem with the choices you make. Your words and accusations are becoming too bitter. You only seem to panic when it's too late and I'm giving up. But this pull and push game leaves me exhausted. It's not in my interest to be with someone who shows so much hate, that sees things in me that are not even part of my personality, that smiles with joy when I'm mad, and even says that it's funny to see me mad, that is deliberately destroying the relationship while asking me questions to justify blaming me for it. And I can't be making efforts alone all the time. I like you a lot, but you're not smart, even for yourself. And I don't see how can you enjoy calling friends to those who believe you are dumb. It seems like you have no sense of right and wrong, and need to hurt yourself to understand such difference. I'm even realizing now that you've become def to my words. Whatever I say doesn't matter to you anymore. That makes me lose trust on you. And love without trust means little. But everyone owns their own freewill. I told you this from the start: We can be together for as long as you want, we didn't met for a short term relationship, but you have freewill to destroy it if you decide it.

I was extremely careful with you from the start, but I had no idea that you would deliberately destroy something that you, at the same time, wanted to have. There was a period in which you said, "I'm sorry", but now, you laugh about it, and cry when I breakup with you. There was a period in which I didn't have to say anything and you would be careful enough not to damage the relationship, but now, you ask me what I want and then do the opposite. You're clearly expecting me to finish things. Gloria, you need to be discarded several times until you realize what love is, but by then, however, you will be so screwed that you won't find anyone who loves you back anymore. You're too young to manifest cognitive dissonance at the level you show, and I worry about you because I love you. But I don't know how to reach you anymore. It feels like I lost you already. You have decided to crash and burn.

At first, our relationship made sense, because there are things about us that others can't see, and many things about you that nobody knows. I doubt that any of your friends really knows you. But maybe I'm just being too optimistic here. Now, you're making sure that the differences go beyond your personality, just to see if you can destroy the relationship on purpose. However, you cry every time I breakup with you and blame me for doing it, after causing every single one of our breakups yourself and on purpose, just to test my limits. You don't know what you're doing, your friends don't help you, and I'm being as patient as it is humanly possible. I'm exhausted as well. I did the mistake of assuming that you would be making efforts to keep the relationship, but now feels like I'm dealing with a child in a woman's body.

ROWAN KNIGHT

You know Gloria, you always make me angry, by telling me that what is expensive has more quality. Well, guess what! You are far more expensive than your real value. The cost of being with you is too high for the crap I have been taking from you. You should be the one making efforts to be with me. Not the opposite! You have nothing to offer me. You are toxic and evil. In essence, you're just waiting for a better guy to come along, and that's why you behave like a 5yo. That's why guys have sex with you and leave you. You don't have value to anyone, except as a sexual object. I'm the stupid one for wanting more. You're not that type of woman. You are not wife or girlfriend material. You are whore material only. If you behave like one, that's what you really are.

You also contradict yourself all the time, and I mean, in the same day you said you didn't love me, you invited me to visit your hometown and meet your parents, book vacations with you for up to the following five months, and you even started crying when I said that I didn't want to be with you. Now you cry all the time when I'm breaking up. But you're getting worse. Are you insane? At least my previous girlfriends fought over babies and marriage, but you fight because I don't get drunk and don't go camping with you, and because there are no butterflies in your stomach. Seriously? Go catch the butterflies and eat them to see if you can feel them.

Maybe you're really with me just because of sex, as you said once. Or maybe you simply need a boyfriend to validate yourself, as other guys just want to have sex with you and leave you. No wonder, as you have no value as a woman. You're a baby in a woman's body. And yet, I can't really tell if you're more childish or more abnormal. What kind of freak, shares her bed with a gay man that sleeps naked every night? That is not normal. I still can't believe this is the life you had before I met you. That was the first time I realized you have serious mental problems. I only changed my mind about not leaving you in that moment because you quickly moved in to my house. You must have realized I was going to quit on you after noticing that circus.

Marrying you crossed my mind many times, until you decided that you're entitled to sleep wherever you want, when you want it. You're not qualified to marry anyone. You are qualified to live like a slut only. Your own mother expects her 23yo daughter to be single all of her life. That's a lot for a young woman! But I guess your mother must really know you super well. I'm only now starting to agree with her. I can give you another chance but I don't know how long it will last before you start another fight."

The Jealousy Games

One of Gloria's sex buddies came back from Russia to see her, and she thought that it's normal to go meet with our friends in the same bar where he was waiting for her. Instead of avoiding him, Gloria allowed him to put his hands on her and didn't even do anything to stop him. Again, she challenged me, and disrespected me, in front of many people, probably trying to create a fight...

Adam: — "Why do you talk to you ex-boyfriend and why do you even allow him to touch you?"

Gloria: — "I do whatever I want. You can't stop me from talking to other people. If you cannot handle it, it's your problem."

Adam: — "In that case, you can leave the apartment, as I never wanted to live with such slutty woman. I said that you are free to do what you want with your life, I said that a relationship requires constant efforts and I said that you don't behave like most women in relationships and therefore I can't trust you to be alone, or drunk and alone. You are incapable of pushing a guy away when he puts his hands on you, you are incapable of prioritizing your relationship over random guys hitting on you and you enjoy freedom and one night stands, which, sorry to tell you, is not normal. What I saw made me sick. If you think I have to be the one changing for you to keep doing such things, you are totally wrong. I don't have to and won't tolerate that. You won't party alone or sleep somewhere else again without me. And I don't want to even see you near guys you had sex with or receiving their messages. If this is too much for you, you can leave me. I told you that I want a serious relationship with someone. I can't be the one always fixing your mistakes. You either want a new life or the previous. I'm not the one who has to adapt to you. I've done a lot already and even found an apartment like you wanted."

Gloria: — "You always keep saying that you're fed up of me, and you're always offending me by calling me stupid, and you keep repeating that you made a mistake. Why do you want to live with a mistake? And I don't see anything bad with what I did. I didn't talk with that guy. Just because I did not push him the way you wanted, drama begun. And you cannot tell me that I am not going to party alone with friends anymore. And after you ask what kind of worries I have. It is obvious ones. I just brought my luggages and dunno if to pack or take everything and leave. So in this case you are not being consistent."

Adam: — "You want to be in a relationship where you can do whatever you want, sleep where you want, party alone and talk to different guys trying to have sex with you after a few beers, without caring about the feelings of another person, right? So I think you have chosen the wrong man to play this game. We're always fighting about the same thing: Your selfishness! If you don't like men that complain, then you must like men that use you and abandon you, because they all see the same."

Gloria: — "You are just assuming. Yeah, of course, I just want to fuck with any random guy. I'm clapping for you for those words. Keep thinking like that, and after it's easier for you to explode when someone even talks to me."

Adam: — "I have told you the rules to be in a relationship with me. They apply to any woman. Most women already know them without being told. I said in the beginning that I could help you experience the relationship. I said we can be very happy together. But I also said you have the power to destroy everything. If you can't accept these rules, then you can't accept me. Because maybe your type is actually someone that does to you the same things you do to others. If you want to be with me, you respect me. If you want to be selfish, then it's better you continue experiencing your life like a teenager. I think it was a mistake to be in a relationship with you."

Gloria: — "Oh, so if you made a mistake, you can easily quit it."

Adam: — "Fine... I quit!"

Gloria: — "Well done!"

Gloria started crying...

Gloria: — "Please Adam, don't breakup with me. I will do anything you ask. I promise I will change my behavior and show more respect for you."

DESTINY: WHEN YOUR SOULMATE FINDS YOU

I softened with Gloria's supplications. But days later another argument begun, this time because she wanted to meet with a friend that I never heard about:

Adam: — "Can I go meet her with you?

Gloria: — "No! She's my friend, not yours. We are going to talk girl's things."

Adam: — "Where will you meet her?"

Gloria: — "I don't have to tell you that."

Adam: — "Then if you go meet with your friend, the relationship is over. Because if you have always behaved like a slut, and still talk and act like a slut, I have to behave like I'm dealing with a slut, in short, without any trust on you. I did offer you an engagement ring on your birthday, which was really expensive to me, and because you asked me for it, but everything comes with a price. If you want a marriage, you must deserve it..."

Gloria: — "What the hell are you talking? She wants to meet me, because we didn't meet on my birthday and today there is a concert in a summer terrace where there will be a performance of my favorite Lithuanian singer. And Camilla will join us. But I am forbidden to meet my friends. Ok then, just lock me in the box."

Adam: — "First, you lied when saying it was just a drink in a bar and not a concert. Then, you lied again, when saying it was only you and her and not mentioning Camilla. And you lied once more, when telling me that you didn't know where it was, which you do, if it's a concert you're attending. You refused to let me be there, but I don't trust you and I have no reasons to trust you, and the more you provoke and lie, the less I trust you. You have guys crossing the planet just to have sex with you, you keep communicating with ex-boyfriends and other guys, but my life is not a joke and I told you exactly this last time we had a fight. I also said you shouldn't live with me if you can't handle the pressure. If that is the case, you can go back to your previous life before you met me. You don't trust me, but you're the one that is not trustworthy and is putting absolutely no efforts to be trusted. You did not just move in with me. I'm not your roommate and I don't care about what your idiotic friends think of me or say. You are the kind of woman that allows men to put their hands on you without complaining about it. The kind of woman that sleeps with strangers as if it was just another beer in the night. I do not trust you and I don't have to trust you. I won't tolerate that you meet people alone and behind my back. I don't have to. I think your body moved to this new house, but your brain remained in the loft where you lived before. You still don't understand do you?"

Gloria: — "No, I don't. Should I tell you every word of what I talk to my friends? Camilla just wrote me where is the concert and she wants to go, so I invited my friend to join her. I don't need to immediately update you on that. Everybody had one night stands, and you are blaming me for that, even if you had it as well. To fuck with any random guy every day is selling your body and soul, but to have free one night stands when you are single, I don't see a tragedy here. I regret telling you about my past or everything else, because you step on it. You treat me as a whore. You are the dumb one who expects a whore to change. I did not want you to join, because we go only with girls; she is not inviting her boyfriend as well, you know."

Adam: — "I don't need to predict the future of someone who says what you just did. You see, I didn't end this relationship more than five times before. On the contrary, I gave you more than five opportunities to change. And last time we talked, you promised you would, and from what you say now it was a lie."

Gloria: — "Wow, a hero! Did not end the relationship more than five times and gave me opportunities. Yeah, you can state like this, that you want to end the relationship all the time, so the number will increase. Every time shit happens, you want to break up. If you are pissed just because I didn't clean the kitchen, you immediately want to break up."

Adam: — "Your sarcasm tells me that I shouldn't have listened to you that day, when you said you didn't want to end the relationship and would make efforts to change. You're actually saying that your ex-boyfriends did well when abandoning you without giving you a second chance. So why do you live with me? Need a better roommate? It also tells me that you are a selfish and immature person, and not interested in a relationship. The kitchen actually looks like a shit today and I didn't say anything, so that's called paranoia. And no, I don't break up every time shit happens, because shit doesn't just happen. You create it. And the more you talk like this, the worse it makes you look like, and the more you prove me right. That's why I have to put rules on you. If you don't like them, you're free to go back to the life you had. You are wrong if you think that I will adapt to your behavior. My rules are clear: If you meet people behind my back, it's over. I have no reasons to trust you, and no intentions to get hurt again in my life. Do you know why all of your friends say that we don't match? Because I'm too honest and serious, and you're the opposite, you have no self-respect, and you make yourself look worse when you take pride on your behavior. The reason why most of your friends like you, is because you make them feel good when making yourself look bad. I don't like to walk around knowing that dozens of guys in the city slept with the woman next to me but were smarter than me in not entering a relationship with her. You must be insane, if you think that this is normal. And you must be hallucinating if you think you will continue insulting me and not see this relationship ending faster than what you imagined."

The Social Masks

Adam: — "You are quite skillful at changing your attitude depending on who you're with. It is as if you had a huge collections of masks, one for each occasion. I'm always impressed, at how well you can adapt to each one of your masks. Besides, there's no consistency in you, and you don't even know who you are, as you said it yourself too. No wonder, with all those transitions in your personality. I don't really know what you do with your life, with whom you go out with, and what you do outdoors, behind my back. And taking into consideration your past, I can't trust you either. Besides, I see you texting with guys all the time, sometimes near me, and the more I confront you with this, the more you provoke; and the more you provoke, the more you reveal your true nature. You even said that I deserve to be cheated. I didn't know the whole picture when I met you, and you did promise to change, which you clearly can't. And that's why I started putting a bunch of rules on you. However, you do not understand anything, you can't tell right from wrong, and you don't like to follow rules. You also didn't move in with me to change roommate. There are implications, and the more you provoke me, the worse it is for you. These phrases are not from someone who wants to be in a relationship:

- "The guys hit on me because you don't behave like my boyfriend";

- "Guys hit on me and touch me, and I let them because I don't want to be rude";

- "I never wanted a guy like you; We don't match; You are boring".

On top of this, you want to party all night long and sleep on other people's house. But last time I wanted to go in a club on my own you said, "I don't want you to go". You are also super paranoid whenever I'm writing on my mobile, even though you reply to all the guys texting you.

I don't think you have the capacity to understand what a relationship is. You are just playing a game with my life. You always want a new chance, promising to change, but then you behave as always. Sometimes I'm walking with you on the street and you even stare at some random guy and smile while waiting for him to notice you. They always ignore you, but how does that make me feel, when you stare at a guy you had sex with while holding hands like my life is a puppet show? It's like you want them to say hello to you and notice that you have a boyfriend, that you're not some random slut. And when I ask who are they, you then reply "nobody" or, "one of my female's friend". You may lie a lot about the exact number of strangers you had sex with, but it is clear already that, in just one year, you had sex with a Chilean, a Lithuanian, a Spanish, a Romanian and two Portuguese. You said it yourself. And that's too much! Feels like I'm with a common prostitute. You even admitted that we could have had sex easily if I wanted, in the second night after I arrived, because that's all you wanted from me. But worse than that, is when you admitted to have sex without protection with strangers, without any consideration for sexually transmitted diseases.

You fear that I may go back to my ex-girlfriends, and meanwhile you're the one texting with yours. You ask me every day to which coffee shop I'm going, and when I ask you once where is the bar where you're having beers with friends, you make a terror tantrum like I have no right to know. You want to spend weekends partying, but when I tell you that I may stay a month outside the country, you freakout and complain. You also create terror tantrums whenever I stop you from spending the entire night drunk in some club with I don't know who, and when I complain about you sleeping in I don't know where. I don't even know why you want the relationship, as it doesn't make any sense. You are a slut, you behave like one, you act like one and you complain like one.

Meanwhile, I prepare your homework for English classes, I cook you dinner all the time, I tell you where I'm going and with who, I ask you to join,... I must be the biggest sucker you ever met. That's why you like me so much. It's the perfect combination — a total idiot with enough money to support you and pay for your expenses and addictions, while you spend your money whoring yourself in clubs and getting drunk.

Last night, I even cooked dinner for both of us, and for your lunch today, and then prepared your homework, and even wrote two texts for you to choose the one you like the most, and you didn't even wash the dishes. At the same time, I took care of the laundry, as you're too lazy for that as well. Your excuse for leaving the house like a trashcan is always "I didn't feel like it". You actually laid in bed scrolling on your mobile and texting with friends while I did all these things. But worse than witnessing this, is your complete lack of empathy. On the morning of the 23th of May 2017, I went with you to work on a bicycle. You were behind me, riding yours. At some point, while crossing the bridge, you started screaming and I thought you were in trouble, looked back to see what was happening, lost control, fell down, scratched my whole hands and arms, and hurt my right arm, which I can't move properly since. But how can I explain to you, that you should, at least, apologize? Despite what you might think, normal people do not scream like you did, do not cause accidents, and when they do, they can apologize. Do you know what could have happened because of your stupid behavior Gloria? I could have fallen on the side of the road and get my head smashed by a car. And do you know why I even looked back? Because I thought you were in danger when screaming like a maniac. Should I just continue and let you fall down from the bridge or get attacked by someone? And what if it was car accident heading your way? Your friend didn't scream like you, even if you were screaming because you found her. I was only hearing your voice, because other people are not like you. What you see as funny, is not funny, is just you being the idiot you are. You are so irresponsible that you make a responsible person take more risks than necessary because of you, because you behave like a child. I hurt my arm, I got a bunch of scars, not to hit with my head on the floor, and you think that I looked back because I'm dumb? Maybe one day you will scream again, like a maniac, and I will ignore you, and you will just die. Your only concern was that I screamed at you in front of your friend. Should I be the one saying sorry to you? You even said that studying and doing therapy on yourself was a waste of money that you could use on beer. Gloria, this relationship has to end. I believe that it is better to solve things like this than having my hand flying towards your face, which is what you ask for."

Gloria: — "Ahahah! You really need to see a psychiatrist. Why you complain about me to your friends? Why don't you say to them that you are physically abusive and threaten to break my face?"

Adam: — "Good luck in finding a man that accepts you Gloria! I'm not that person. My life is not your joke!"

Gloria: — "A mental hospital would help. You are putting yourself in a jokers situation. And now you even complain to my friends. Nice!"

Adam: — "They are not your friends. They are friends of the mask you put in front of them. They don't know who you are. And I don't deserve less respect than them. A rather live on my own than with you. Besides, trying to prove me insane, just makes you look worse than you already are. You are evil, selfish, egotistical and mean. I have seen what you can do. Nothing has changed. You entered my life to destroy it. Nothing else!"

Gloria: — "How can I say sorry to you, when you immediately started shouting at me. You have mental problems. I see no results from your efforts."

Adam: — "And you never will. That's why I don't want to be with you. I already did what I could by loving you. You are lost. I just wish you didn't destroy my life as you did. We went from you saying, "I always behave like this in my relationships" to "It's all your fault". And from saying, "I promise I will change and I know I have a problem to solve", to "It's all your fault that the relationship doesn't work". The Gloria you show me is the same one I know from the start. These mind games of trying to shift guilt towards me make you look pathetic. It is your fault that the relationship doesn't work, otherwise you wouldn't put so many efforts to prove me wrong."

Gloria: — "I hope I won't find anyone who always humiliates his girlfriend."

Adam: — "The more you talk and provoke, the more you prove me right. You cannot change or promise changes, because you are sick. You even tell me that my problem is knowing too much."

Gloria: — "I may go tomorrow in my hometown, because my sister with her baby came back. Do you want to go?

Adam: — "No! We are over."

DESTINY: WHEN YOUR SOULMATE FINDS YOU

After this Gloria disappeared and went out to party with her friends. At midnight I went to sleep, and at 3AM she arrived home drunk, making a huge noise when opening the door. She went straight to bed and woke me up...

Adam: — "Where have you been?"

Gloria: — "It's none of your business."

Adam: — "My house is not a shelter for sluts. You do not go out to fuck whenever you have "sexual needs" as you said before, and arrive home after midnight without an explanation. I'm not your father. First, you move out, then you can go to hell. If your problem is money, sell the commitment ring I gave you on your birthday, because it was not intended for a woman that only thinks of herself. I'm not going to correct the education your parents clearly failed in giving you."

Gloria: — "If I say I want you to leave the house?"

Adam: — "Do you think my life is a joke, and I can just buy and cancel flights and hotels whenever I want?"

Gloria: — "I don't care. You think I can just pack my whole things and go rent in a hotel? You humiliate me a lot. And you know I don't have how to transfer everything. And you know that I don't have enough money for those things. And you know I need to move out from the loft as well. I rented it because of you, and now I'm ending up with no place to live."

Adam: — "Ask the guy you had sex with to help you and complain to him."

Gloria: — "Idiot."

Adam: — "And next time you reply online to travelers looking for pussy in Vilnius, like Andreas and others, don't forget to include your price. You can have two things you want so much: Uncommitted sex with strangers and lots of money to pay for the expenses when nice guys breakup with you upon realizing you're just a stupid selfish bitch. You can sell the ring I offered you for extra cash or prostitute yourself if you want, instead of just offering free pussy. The room you should be renting is in a psychiatric hospital."

Gloria: — "Fuck off!"

Adam: — "Taking you to a psychologist was my last attempt at doing something for you. Now, I'm ready to restart my life from zero to let you go. Your friends win. You are only good drunk. Your family wins. You are better when ignored. I lose. I can't love anyone like you."

On the following day, Gloria packed her things...

Gloria: — "I have packed. Will take out my stuff on Sunday."

Adam: — "Where will you go? Your last night fuck-buddy offered you a bed?"

Gloria: — "I did not have sex with anyone. My best friend came back from the United Kingdom, I was with her, and her friends."

Adam: — "For the past months, you have tortured me in a variety of ways, offended me multiple times, and then you asked, when I complained: "Why are you with me if you think I'm evil?"

This reminds me of a story: A snake was hit by a car. A woman picks her up, feeds her and gets her to full state of health. But then the snake bites her, injecting her with deadly poison. On her death bed, she asked: "After all I did, why me?", to which the snake responded: "You knew I was a snake when you picked me up."

Your insults are poisonous, your provocations are poisonous,... you are like a poisonous snake. The arrogance and pride you show me in being like a poisonous snake makes you who you are. But I did not invite a snake to live with me to be poisoned to death.

You want me to be violent to place yourself as a victim, instead of aggressor. But I don't want to play that game with you. I told you from the start that I was going to go the whole way with you. I did. You got a house, a ring (that actually means much more than what you think) and an opportunity to fix yourself and become a better person, better than anyone that knows you could ever imagine. I gave you a chance to prove to anyone you know that they were wrong about you. I gave you a chance to completely change your life and yourself. And I even offered you a chance to quit your job and never have to work again for the rest of your life. But that path is over now. You have ended it. I've already went the whole way. I can't save you from yourself. Only you save yourself."

Gloria: — "You are being selfish now. I have no money anymore and I have no place to stay. You are making me now have to spend more than I even have. I have a provoking personality, but did not expect these things from you. You hurt me so much. You are the first person in my life with such an interesting personality, and I doubt I will find someone like you, but you are the first one calling me names, offending me, and being physically abusive."

DESTINY: WHEN YOUR SOULMATE FINDS YOU

Adam: — "Emotionally abusive women that refuse to end a relationship are the cause of physically abusive men. You asked me nonstop questions about my previous relationships when I met you, and afterwards too, and then you decided to replicate the same story for me, and do what others did. For what? To torture me? To prove that I'm evil? To make me evil? I have more fights with you than I ever had with anyone else before. And you don't change. My former girlfriends never got even a ring, but they stopped drinking beer because of me and became vegetarian too for me. The fights happened because they wanted a baby and to get married, and I didn't want to marry them or have a son with them. You have no idea how jealous they would be of you.

I tried to end my last relationship many times, for five years. She didn't allow it. She would stay at my door, crying the whole night, until I open it, even if it was in the morning, when I went to work. If she couldn't enter the building where I lived, she would stay outside, in the snow, freezing, just to catch me when I arrived. I had no idea whatsoever of how to get rid of her. I was exhausted with everything. In the end, when we moved from China to Thailand, I simply abandoned her when I got the chance, and left our apartment in Thailand to move to Spain, while she was traveling in the United States. And yet, I had told her several times that I was going to leave her. She simply didn't believe anymore, and thought she could continue insulting me forever. That might have been the longest relationship I ever had but was also the only violent one. You did a very grave mistake in trying to replicate it with me.

You lack the maturity of a woman, but also the discipline and responsibility of someone who wishes to work for me and under my rules. You're the kind of person that, the worse things get, the worse you make them. I never really had a chance to fix anything. You don't know how to keep self-respect, you don't keep the distance with other men, you accept whatsoever people tell you about me, and you have a weak opinion of what you want, and of the relationship. But instead of building trust, you provoke me more, and it kills the relationship when you do it. Yes, you may have to refuse going to concerts. Yes, you may have to abdicate from that summer festival, in which you get drunk for three days with friends and camp with whomever you want. But if one day you want to be married, you better start realizing the meaning of trust in a relationship, because you step a lot on it. I don't want to see you drunk anymore or partying alone. I really don't. You can't deal with drinks, you always get drunk. You don't get to choose what you want to do when it hurts another person and damages the relationship. You either want love in the relationship or you want to love a bottle of alcohol. One has to go. Responsibility and saying sorry is not difficult. However, you rarely say it. But better than saying sorry, is accepting responsibility.

I also know that, without me, your life is heading in a very different direction, with concrete karmic consequences. If you choose the life direction you have with me, you will abdicate of drinking alcohol or eating meat for the rest of your life. You will abdicate from going out with anyone whenever I'm not present. You will receive therapy to solve your problems. In those sessions, you will cure the direct cause behind your aggressions towards me. You won't smoke weed ever again, or anything else for that matter, including a single cigar. If you do these things, I will marry you within a year or two. After two years, you can quit your job, and you can start living the life you always dreamed of, traveling the world with me, and even consider having your own family, including your first baby. You can actually be very happy. But if you decide to push me apart, to be with your friends, you will end up in a room, after leaving our house, and go back to your previous routines, of partying every weekend with friends until you are totally wasted. You may go back to smoking weed as well, and to have one night stands with strangers. But the hallucinations you started having recently, of seeing faces on paintings moving and turning into demons, will appear more often to you. Your nightmares, related to death and murder, will repeat themselves more often as well. You will feel more lonely and more depressed than ever before. In despair, you will have sex with strangers more often, you will smoke weed more often, and start drinking more often too, in order to forget your misery. You will ruin your soul furthermore. And one day, someone, maybe one of your roommates, will open the door of your room and find you dead in bed, with bottles of alcohol next you. I won't be in this last reality for sure. And the only way for you to choose the second option, and live, is if I reenter your life. Would that happen?"

Pushing The Boundaries of The Relationship

It is obvious that Gloria didn't just say, "You saved me", several times and shortly after we started this relationship for no reason, as it is clear for me now that I didn't just fell in love for a person that I knew from the start that I should be avoiding. I did fell in love with Gloria to save her, and I couldn't fight that back, despite trying hard to avoid thinking of her every single day and avoiding what I felt, especially, when we were apart after our breakups. Gloria, however, kept pushing the boundaries...

Adam: — "Gloria, why did you went and told everyone in your family that I'm physically abusive?

Gloria: — "I told what happened between us, the situation. I was not justifying myself. I was just crying a lot. So my mom was reacting, and after that I got over it, and explained everything. But my brother that knows me, even said that I am this kind of personality that pisses off. I told my mom that you have more good qualities than bad, and I need to fix myself. She likes you, Adam. I am sorry for that, but could not hold the tears in front of my family."

Adam: — "You basically made me react aggressively so that you could have something to use to clean your reputation in front of others. I didn't want to be with you after that night. And especially after you repeatedly said, "Hit me!""

Gloria: — "Enough, Adam!"

Adam: — "I don't like this kind of game you created of "He has more good qualities than bad". That is you manipulating others to make yourself look good. You know Gloria, you wanted to prove that I have mental problems, and for what? Do you think a psychiatrist will cure me and then I can be next to you, passive, while you provoke me? There's no cure for someone that is reacting to an emotionally and psychologically abusive woman. That is exactly why I broke up with you. That's what I want you to understand."

Gloria: — "Why are you starting it again?"

Adam: — "What you did by spreading to your family that I'm aggressive is horrible. I'm not starting it again Gloria. It's simply not over. You used me. You spread to your friends and family that I beat you. You used me to clean your reputation."

Gloria: — "No, I said the truth. I was hurt. Even if I provoked."

Adam: — "You made me look bad in front of everyone to clean your reputation, so that later you can say, "We broke up because he beats me", when in fact that's bullshit. We broke up many times because you insult me for months. You manipulated me first, and then you used me to manipulate others. You didn't want to admit that the relationship failed because of you, so you had to say it was because I attacked you, when in fact you insulted me the whole day, arrived home in the afternoon totally drunk, and then took the blanked from me, kicked me and said, "I won't let you sleep". Did you said this to them as well? I bet you didn't. You just said, "I provoked him" to make yourself look like the victim.

What you did when visiting your family just made everything worse, because I have no way of looking at them ever again. Did you say to them, "I was totally drunk when I provoked him, and laughed at his face, and made fun of him, and didn't let him sleep at 4AM, and he hit me back like anyone would in such situation?" Did you say this? Of course you did not. You said, "I just provoked, and he attacked me, but he has good qualities too".

Do you know how many times I have seen this movie before? You are an expert in the art of manipulating others. I won't ever visit any of your family members again. I have no way of looking at them after what you did. And if you think you are in a relationship with an abusive man, and you are a helpless victim, then you've just justified the reason behind all breakups, although distorted to your side. This fight in which I punched your arm is not even from now. You brought it back to justify the last breakup, instead of telling them that I fell from the bike and got angry because you didn't apologize and instead decided to put a party in the house and sing at 10PM. And after that you arrived drunk at 3AM and said: "It's none of your business where I spend the night". Did you tell them this too? Did you tell them what you did on the night before you met them? I bet you did not. When your brother says that you provoke too, he is not even seeing the whole picture. You devalued me in front of your family to protect your image. We didn't have normal fights and normal breakups, and I'm not violent. You are not in an abusive relationship. You are sick and you don't want anyone to know.

Now I understand why your mother asked you yesterday if I was waiting for you with a dinner. You surely told her that you broke up with me because I beat you and not the opposite. It's the most insane thing I have ever seen."

Gloria: — "We can talk about it later."

Adam: — "You spent a whole year pushing me away, not knowing what you want, blaming me for being the opposite of what you wanted, and for not being the type of guy you were looking for. And yet, I'm afraid you still don't know what you want, you still don't like who you have and you're still looking for someone else, reason why you keep provoking me all the time. I think you are changing, but towards the old you. Many of the accusations you made, actually match you. You demand a lot, but you give nothing back."

Gloria: — "Where do you get things like that I am still looking for someone else?"

Adam: — "I think today you can say one thing and even believe what you say, and tomorrow you will do something else and justify it, just as you have always done it. You are too obsessed with your own needs, and you're not ready for a relationship. You were not ready before and you may never be. I don't see it as part of your nature. You have already formed your personality. It's too easy for you to sleep with anyone but it's impossible for you to commit to one. It's too easy for you to do whatever you want, but impossible for you to obey and follow someone else. It's too easy for you to know nothing about yourself and not care, but too difficult to make plans, be responsible and commit to a future. I think the demands you pass on me are disguised by guilt and hidden behind a confusion of values. And I feel like I am more a choice of your family than a choice of yours. You don't want a guy like me. It doesn't seem so."

Gloria: — "Adam, I just really don't know what is the answer you are looking for. Don't say I don't care, because I put also a lot of efforts. And your sentence about obeying, I am not sure if a relationship should be about that."

Adam: — "I built a very clear and straightforward path for you to follow. You are the one that refused it. And when you say that I use you for company, it seems to me the opposite is what happens. I don't know how you interpret your efforts or what kind of efforts you are referring to. I need to know the difference between the Gloria who sleeps with any guy, and tells me she needs sex (to justify inviting hundreds of guys to her bed), the Gloria that shared a house of lies with me, while partying, getting drunk, smoking weed, and behaving as if I was a stupid idiot that had to wait for her and accept her selfish behaviors, the Gloria you are now, which I don't know anymore who is, and the Gloria you intend to be, which I have no idea either.

You know Gloria, whenever I want to know something about you, I either get a lie, or a bullshit answer that makes me go around in circles until I forget about the purpose of the question. And I truly believe that as soon as you get the opportunity, you will depart with someone else. But you've made me very tired with these mind-games. You have learned very well how to be a liar. For a young person of your age, you lie too well. But you've never learned how to be honest. The more you know me, the more you practice how to escape questions and lie. And I don't like that.

You've complained a lot about me expelling you from the house, but you should instead ask yourself why should anyone want to share a house with a liar, a dishonest person that is completely addicted to validation from the opposite gender and likes to flirt with men to know how pretty she is, as if guys hitting on her were more important than the one she has.

You are not fit for any relationship. And you may never be. But how can anyone know that (and not just me) if you bluntly refuse to answer anything? I only have your actions to judge. But I don't like to play the fool. And that's how I feel with you.

The psychologist you found made you worse. And along that road, you won't find me anymore. The only reason why you paid her four times is because you were enjoying learning about manipulation and control, so that you could use it against me, as you perfectly know you were never under that situation. To blame me for being emotionally abusive is like dick slapping me with a smile in your face and call me childish when I get mad. There are many things about you that are just difficult for anyone to believe."

Gloria: — "Adam, if you don't see any purpose in the relationship or you don't even think I am a relationship person, I cannot force you to believe. I am letting you choose to have a break."

DESTINY: WHEN YOUR SOULMATE FINDS YOU

Adam: — "You started by living with me, and you have removed yourself step by step. Do you want to go back to my life or you are just waiting for me to leave?"

Gloria: — "First option."

Adam: — "I know you are still too young to understand certain things, but you are not too young to answer for the misbehaviors and lies you tell. It requires a lot of energy and patience to handle you. But answering my questions helps build that trust, especially if you wish to reenter my life. I need to know if you can live with me. I should not even talk to you after finding out that you are getting rides from other men. Some things will never change. And I think the only reason why I get mad is because I expect you to be someone you can't be. That's who you are. You like to fuck different guys, smoke weed and party until you drop drunk in your bed. Anything that requires you being normal just doesn't fit in."

Gloria: — "You talk as if I was smoking everyday. Seriously, you are mad because the driver was a male. You talk as if we were hitting on one another. It was not a date ride that you could talk like that. Nobody forced you to be with me either, Adam. What is your point in talking about the same things after so many months? If I didn't tell you that I love you for half a year, is because it takes time for me. This was not love from the first sight if you want to know that. I was honest. You say I was a waste of time, but you stayed. So why do you kept wasting your time if you knew it was a waste? It's unbelievable you still say this. I smoked weed already almost a year ago, and you still say, 'oh, you probably smoke weed', 'oh your life goal is just to smoke'. When was the last time you saw me drunk for you to still say that I like to be drunk all the time? My one night stands was not after I started to be with you for you to talk so much about it. I don't talk about your one night stands because I don't care, so why the hell you are so attached to mine?"

Adam: — "A man works for sex. A woman only needs to open her legs and choose which one she wants to fuck with. That makes a woman that has many one night stands, a slut by default. Now, one that invites hundreds of guys to sleep with her, because she "needs sex" and "can't live without sex", as you told me, she can call herself a nymphomaniac, although a nymphomaniac is always a prostitute. Not accepting money doesn't change the nature of the act. And don't put it in my face as if I was forced to accept it, just because you think you can fuck whoever you want and then you can marry one idiot of your choice. Nobody wants to have a prostitute for a wife. Especially, if she is a nymphomaniac. And that's what you've shown me with your obsession for strangers in front of me. Of course, I will never believe in "rides with strangers". I will never believe anything a liar tells me. Liars lie, that's what they do."

Gloria never changed despite her promises. Days later, she would push me away to end the relationship, and party with her friends again. She said that I am too old and too ugly for her, and that she wants someone else, better than me. So I ended the relationship and then traveled to Ukraine. Gloria took the chance to party the whole month with her friends, and I was seeing her photos on social media, from the distance, in which she was always completely drunk dancing by herself in clubs every single weekend. And, just as if I was nobody in her life, as if our conversations meant nothing to her, she started using dating apps and meeting with new men too, and as soon as I left. In doing so, she ended a cycle in our relationship. But as mentioned previously, this represented a path without me, and the karmic end of it would have to be death.

Did I Save Her Life?

I missed Gloria, I didn't like my experience in Ukraine, and I returned to Vilnius to see her again, but she didn't seem happy to see me...

Adam: — "Why are you so angry if you don't love me and never did?"

Gloria: — "Because I do love you!"

Adam: — "Why did you try to find another boyfriend if you love me?"

Gloria: — "You left, you left the country. I was super mad at you and thought I should move on without you."

Adam: — "I invited you to my house to marry you. You were trying to find a boyfriend while sharing it."

Gloria: — "I was trying to find after you left. You even said we could be together if I don't have feelings for you."

Adam: — "You said you were trying to find another boyfriend to replace me when we were in the car. That's why I left to Ukraine. You said you enjoyed flirting with other men in front of me, even if it made me look like an idiot. That's why I left to Ukraine. You said you lie to me all the time and it's my fault to believe. That's why I left to Ukraine. You said you deserve better than me. That's why I left to Ukraine. You said I'm too old and too fat for you. That's why I left to Ukraine. You took revenge on your father, former boyfriends, and all the other men that hurt you and abandoned you, by hurting me. You seemed very proud of that as if you had become a successful strong woman by hurting me. You attacked the only man who truly loved you to revenge the others. Your arrogance comes from this false sense of pride. And I need a woman who truly loves me. That's why I left to Ukraine. You said that it's very easy for you to have sex with strangers but not with me because I'm much older and you're not sure if you want to be with me. That's why I left to Ukraine. You never explained these words, you never apologized, you never asked me to stay. You decided to go party with your friends after saying these horrible words. That's why I left to Ukraine. When we fight, I suffer and can't work, but you party and have fun and don't care about me. That's why I left to Ukraine."

Gloria: — "So why did you still came back? Then what do you want from me?"

Adam: — "I want to marry you and build a family with you. The amount of words I have written you, when in love, anger or simply worried about the relationship's future, words that you did not read and ignored, words you called poems, could fill an entire library. That's care, even though I offered you a library of wisdom you never visited because you found clubbing more interesting for your future and success as a woman. You put the attention of other men as a priority when compared to respecting me. That's why I left to Ukraine. You don't understand me because you never met a real man before. Only boys! You think I'm just another toy like those boys because you're just a little girl. You are afraid to be a woman. You are afraid to grow up. You are afraid of responsibility and life and commitment and compromise and respect and obedience. You are afraid of the world. You want me to want you but you want someone else that doesn't exist. You want to sleep with dozens of men as before to remember that lesson. You want to go back to the toy store with endless shelves of men to play with because you think you are a princess from a fairytale. And you are seeing your life pass you while you waste it partying and living like a school girl in a dorm. We don't match because you are like a child. When people tell you that we don't match they are offending you, not me. When they say you found a sugar daddy, they are again offending you and not me, because it's like calling you useless by associating yourself with a guy that owns businesses and has much more knowledge about life than they do. When your friends say that I'm too serious, they are again calling you dumb and immature. Can't you see that? Can't you see that people want you as you are, and not growing up faster? Your friends do not want you to change, because they know that if your life improves, you will be too busy without them. But you love your friends more than you love me. You listen to them but not me. I took you with me to Spain, France, Portugal and Holland. I shared my house with you. I promised marriage after only three months of dating you. I offered you my own money to live with. How can you be so short-minded and not see all that? Do you really think your friends love you? Who ever loved you more than me? Who ever will for the rest of your life? Where on the whole planet will you find anyone with more knowledge and more care for you? Where on the whole planet will you find someone capable of changing you into a better person? Maybe all you want is parties, beer and roses. Any guy can give you that. If that is what you want, anyone else can be good for you. If that is what you want, any man can be better than me. And when you accuse me of using you for sex, you are putting me below the level of all the other men you had sex with for sex only. I believed you could love me and that's why I did so much for you. That's why I offered you my own life, that took me twenty years to build. Do you understand now my anger? I feel betrayed. I want someone who makes me happy and respects me, and not someone who constantly provokes me and makes me angry. You can party with your friends and meet your friends, but when I meet a friend of mine, you get completely crazy. You don't understand relationships Gloria. If you don't want to be with me or can't, don't blame me for your own life. You built it."

Gloria: — "I know you are better than others in many ways, however, those "losers", as you call them, never touched me or even threatened... that was a huge thing for me. After these things, all your qualities just vanish."

Adam: — "A woman who wants to cheat and make me violent is also a big thing for me. These two things made all other qualities in you vanish. And no, I don't want to see you with another man, as much as you don't want to see me with another woman. Love, respect and trust walk hand in hand. Can't be separated. I became violent because I couldn't end a relationship with someone emotionally abusing me. You created this situation. But you can't see it because the "losers" abandoned you instead of fighting.

You have only two options in life: to trust me or to learn from experience. I told you the stories of my former girlfriends, for you to learn, not for you to copy them. It does not bring me joy to know you will fall into your own traps or to see you sleeping in a dorm again. It does not give me joy to see the person I love failing in life. It may take you a while to realize the truth in what I say. But if you don't trust it, you won't ever see it. Love works in your heart; not in your head. And I am very sorry about the mistakes you did in the past, which destroyed your potential to love, but if you can listen more to your own heart, and less to your mind, you can go through. Everyone dies but few people live.

I can say sorry for being someone I'm not, for being angry and violent. But I don't want a person who cheats, flirts in front of me, and makes me behave like that. My anger and violence is justified. But you can't see that because you fear my hand movements since I met you. I was confused back then. Then I understood why. You are violent with men and you fear their reaction but you can't stop yourself. But Gloria, I hope you can see that this is not the way. The main reason why I sent you out of the house many times is because I did not want the fights. I sent you out not to be violent. Do you understand now? You say, "I am very sorry for the things I said or did. I wish I never told you those things" ...since I started dating you. There was even a time in which you begged me to take you back, promising that nothing bad would ever happen again. But you never stopped. You have been insulting me, provoking me and attacking me since the first day I met you. The first time I dumped you, you even said, "I am always evil to my boyfriends". Then, when everyone started seeing it, you decided to fabricate a story with the help of the psychologist, to portray yourself as a poor victim of domestic abuse, so that your family and friends keep thinking that you are some angel, and it's all my fault. And you won, because I don't want to see any of them anymore. But this violence that you portray, never happened and you know it, despite the fact that you dick slapped me multiple times, attacked me physically as I sleep, laughing like a drunk clown, and provoked me nonstop while saying: "Hit me! Hit me!". You wanted me to hit you because what others think of you is more important than your relationship, or your mental health. You live in a constant horror of what others think of you, but as a famous author said once: "I pity those who suffer and humiliate themselves for the approval of others because they are truly stupid."

You don't seem sorry when you do the things you do, because, immediately after, you run to party with your dear friends Marius, Ramune and Samantha. Every time we had a fight, for two years, you partied. And I know, for a fact, that you created many fights on purpose, in order to get the freedom to party with them. You are never sorry for anything you do. How could you be sorry for trying to cheat on me for two years? How can you feel sorry for saying I'm too fat for you, too ugly and "too fucking old"? You are not sorry for anything. You, Gloria, are evil! You are evil since I met you. You are evil for two years, and you will most likely always be evil. And I feel sad for you, and very sorry,

but I cannot help you anymore. You are an adult. You are responsible for the consequences of your actions. You are responsible for my anger and losing the house, and losing the relationship. I was not an angry person when you met me, was I? I always did my best to make you happy. You have been attacking me in the most horrible ways, making me look stupid in front of others, chatting with ex-boyfriends online and in front of me, humiliating me in front of other men, because as you said: "I like the look in their eyes when they want to fuck me." And didn't you say: "It's funny to see you angry"?

Well, I hope you are now rolling all over on the floor laughing about it.

You are not sorry for anything. You are only sorry for yourself, because you can't get what you want. But your life is your responsibility. What you did in the past is your responsibility. And what you say and believe about me is your responsibility too. The truth is that I did for you far much more than I should. You did not deserve such a long relationship with me."

Gloria came to my house the next day, seduced me, and we had sex, after nearly two months apart. After that, she started feeling abdominal pain, and later that night, would call me, to tell me that she was fainting in her room and losing conscience. I told her to call an ambulance. A few hours later she would text me from the hospital, saying that she would have to receive an emergency surgery, because she was bleeding internally, and without that operation could die.

I though I would lose her, and yet, I saved her. I think that if she had sex with someone else, instead of me, she would have nobody to call that night, nobody to tell her to call an ambulance, and my prophecy, of Gloria being found dead in her room in the morning, would have been fulfilled, because she didn't want to call an ambulance as I told her to. She believed it was just a normal menstruation pain. It wasn't. An ovarian cyst had opened. And if she had waited three more hours, she would have completely become unconscious and die.

If we were not together by then, and she survived, she would also spend the following days alone in that hospital, full of tubes coming out of her body, and eating horrible food. But I found her and then spent the entire days, every single day, next to her, while she was recovering. I never abandoned her for a single day, and was the only person visiting her. I also cooked healthy and tasty meals to help her recover faster.

Did she deserve all that? I don't know. Only the future could tell. But the truth is that she got very close to ending up dead at only 24yo. And from what I later read, it was the alcohol abuse in all that partying that she went to after expelling me from her life, that caused that to happen. In other words, she nearly caused her own death, as predicted.

I thought that this traumatic experience would have waken Gloria to the fact that her life can only be saved by my side, and not next to her drinking and partying buddies, but I wasn't completely sure she could see it. I did took her to my house to recover despite what she did behind my back and her words in the past. Only God knows if she was having sex with other men already. She admitted that she was meeting with many, but I forgot all that to focus on her recovery.

Would She Learn With Past Mistakes?

Soon after Gloria's recovery, we would have more fights, this time because she kept pushing on me the opinion of her friends in what regards our relationship, and which did not want us to be together:

Adam: — "You should be aware that my opinion comes first, above the opinion of anyone else. Your friends are worth nothing if I can't accept them and they keep trying to destroy the relationship. It is not me that should accept your friends, Gloria. It's the opposite. Any woman who gets married knows that. Your friendship with Samantha, Ramune, and Marius should have ended long time ago. These are not the people you should be partying with or having drinks with. Trust is gained, and you lost it when saying that you tried to cheat on me, when looking at other men in front of me, when doing all the things I mentioned already, when refusing sex with me and saying, "I enjoyed fucking other guys". There is a price to pay for all that. You cannot solve it by saying that it's my fault that I don't forget. And the price is no more partying, ever again, and especially when there are fights, or you will party your end of the relationship with your friends and never see me again. And if you think I manipulate you, you waste my time. In fact, everyone else manipulates you, except me, in case you haven't noticed, because you lack a personality of your own. You want to be a respectful and respected woman? You want to get married and have your own family? Then, you will understand that you must follow what I say. If you cannot accept it, I cannot do anything for you anymore. I am looking for a wife with these characteristics for a long time. If I did not find, is because I spend too much time working and don't have as much time for partying and dating as you do. What relationships should be or not be, what others do or don't do... I don't care.... Because I am not them. I have specific needs and goals in life, and I am looking for a woman to match them. I won't be sleeping with Ramune or Samantha in my bed. I won't have three wives. If I have to keep only one, then she has to be a perfect match to me. Not to other men! I don't live with other men. I don't care about what they do or need. And you make me angry when you compare me with other men, because I am not them. Stop pretending you are a victim to other people, because you're not and you're only dragging yourself down with their words, while pushing me further way with comments, that quite honestly, make you look much worse."

Gloria: — "I need you to be supportive and I will be also. I know I didn't give you attention and we live as roommates because we don't have time for each other, but things will be better, I promise."

Adam: — "How do you know things will get better? How can you promise that, if you don't have any control over your life and always fail to keep any promise? Probably, the worse promises you ever made to me were...

1. When after the first fight ever, you said that you wanted the relationship and were willing to change your behavior, but kept partying, smoking weed, and God only knows what else, like cheating around and kissing other guys. Yeah, I will never forget this year, because your words and actions say more than your promises: carrying around condoms and saying you tried to cheat, in my head means fucking a bunch of guys that didn't want to be your boyfriend and ending with the idiot Adam, as last option, because there's nobody else to keep around and all runaway after sex;

2. When you moved to my house by saying, "I will do anything you ask to stay with you", because things got so violent, I wanted to just leave the country. But you didn't care. You just wanted the house for yourself;

3. When you said that you would do anything for me to stay in the country and not leave, after my flat rental was over. What did I get from that? More of the same! You went on a "psychologist" that is a psycho, and looks more like a mental patient herself, and forever you repeated the mantra: "You are abusive, you are manipulating me, and you are controlling me". Every single time I gave you opportunities, you gave me more abuse in return, and as a result, you kept losing respect for me, because that's what happens when someone like me helps an abusive person like you. And now you look at me like some abandoned dog that you keep around because you have nobody to party with. Only one word from one of your friends, and you are out the door as if I never existed. There is no point in arguing with you. At this point Gloria, I hate myself more than I

hate you, so congratulations on this big achievement of yours. I have seen this movie before, and I am seeing it again, simply because I keep assuming that the end of the movie is different if I keep watching it."

Gloria: — "We broke up, so yes, I did smoke and I did got drunk in January. We were apart, so why should you care?"

Adam: — "If when I close my eyes at night, you do what you want behind my back, then I don't want to see you anymore when I open them in the morning. When I was planning to leave Lithuania, you lied as you always do. You lie about the past, you lie about the future... it is all a lie what comes from you. You lie when you cry, you lie when you smile... you lie when not with me,... you lie when with me. You lie when I care. You lie when I don't care. You lie when you say you won't lie. You will always lie. You are a woman whose nature is to lie. And you told me, before I left Lithuania: "This not who I am, I am not like that". And I stayed, and you behaved as the one you said you are not, because you are a liar. You lie when you suffer, you lie when you are happy, you lie when saying you want a family with me. You lie when you say goodbye. You lie when you cry tears for me not to leave. You cry to get me back. You cry when I put you out of the house, and it means nothing to you. You lie so much you became insane. You lie so much, that you don't even know when you lie to yourself. You can get drunk, smoke weed and sleep with other guys, and lie about everything. You admitted you were looking for a better guy while living in my own house, because you were not sure you wanted the relationship. For a whole year, you were not sure? It was all a lie. When did the relationship start for you? Five months ago? You cannot be trusted apart, under my roof, with me, without me, with words or in silence. Whatsoever I say or not say, nothing matters to you. So who do I love? An illusion?"

Gloria: — "If I want, I drink. If I don't want, I don't drink. It's not your concern anymore."

Adam: — "But you want it all the time, you will always want, and you cannot keep your legs closed when you see a man, you cannot say 'no', when you have a chance to get drunk, and you cannot say 'no' to weed. In your brain, you will always find excuses to do whatever you want. "It was once only", "it's the past", "it was a long time ago", "I will not do it again"... the justifications are always the same. But Gloria, it is my concern. If you think I should not care, you never loved me and you still don't. You want me, but you don't want to respect me. You want a relationship but you don't want to commit. You want me to believe you, but you always lie. There is no concept of right and wrong for you. For you, everything goes, and then the rest of the world has to adapt to the consequences of your behaviors. The problem is that I can see the same pattern always showing itself. The only thing you don't confess doing when we were apart, is cheating. But I can clearly see the patterns of your body when you lie, because you lie for a long time already. This is why, when this morning I asked you questions, I got the truth just by looking at you. And it makes me even more mad when you try to hide what I already know just by observing you. You may never confess you cheated on me, but I am sure you did, because you can lie easily about anything else. You are addicted to sex, alcohol and drugs. If you can't stop alcohol and drugs, you can't stop having sex with strangers either. You are an addicted liar. And you have been insulting me this whole time. I don't think you truly realize the gravity of this situation or the things you do. If anything, you should be locked in a mental hospital for life because you are horribly sick and you will keep getting worse. It's true what they say: You can't turn a whore into a lady. "What color was his car?", you asked me. Does failing on the color means I can't prove it? You already indirectly confessed to cheat. You are a zero as a woman. As a club rat, a beer drinking cow, or your friend's dog, you deserve a medal; but for three years in a relationship, you have been nothing more than a slut and an idiot.

I have promised you marriage and a life without a job, but all you wanted was my money. When you realized I was losing it, you decided to check your options by clubbing more and flirting with other guys, and installing dating apps, and planning trips to England to fuck around without anyone knowing. I found a house for you, you dumb whore! You were sleeping in the bed of a gay man during that time, and texting 300 guys a year for casual sex because you couldn't go through more than two weeks with your legs closed. You have no shame? Gloria, you may have a lot of cock offers all your life, but you will not find anyone even close to my value anymore. I only stayed with you for so long because I was hoping for changes. You did change, on the opposite direction. And there are lots of sluts in this world with mental problems that think they are entitled to a valuable man they can step on and cheat on. Your arrogance really doesn't affect me as much as you imagine. You are even getting uglier very fast and you already have the teeth of someone who has been smoking

too much weed. So, I don't know who is giving you an ego boost and making you believe that you are very special but it's not hard to guess the three names anymore. I truly hope you continue along that road and crush against the wall of reality. You've been doing a very good job so far."

Gloria: — "Even if I will not find a person with the values you have, I am looking for happiness. When Viktorija asked me whether I am happy with you, I couldn't say yes. When she asked me if I love you, if I am in love with you, I also couldn't say yes. So I started to question myself, what do I feel for you, or if I feel anything at all. You embrace your values, but you know, I don't care how many books you wrote if you call me stupid and many other names. I don't care if a surgeon bought your books, if you threaten to beat me."

Adam: — "You are a liar since I met you and you will always be a liar and a cheater because what you really want is a boyfriend at home so you don't feel lonely while sleeping with other guys for fun. I don't know with how many men you had sex with but if you can fuck more than ten men before 22yo and fuck anyone who asks you, and if you kissed more than fifty men in two years, I already know your type. All our fights are just about you trying to convince me that I am the stupid guy you were looking for. You were never a girlfriend and I don't want a fuck friend with sexual diseases from other men.

All liars finish the same, and I will not be blocking your karma anymore. If you think your life was painful before you met me, you will be facing a hell of a ride after I'm gone.

You think you are very important, but I know it's a mask. Deep down, you are a fragile little scared creature, that can't feel anything, doesn't understand anything, is too stupid to keep a valuable relationship, and believes anything her jealous friends say, because you need to get their acceptance, because you are empty — you have no values, no self-respect, no qualities, nothing. You fooled me well when I met you, but now I see who you really are.

Do you know what is really impressive about your insults? I have been trying to keep you apart from people who actually don't like you and think I am better than you. Marius said I'm not your type, because he was comparing a business owner looking for a serious relationship, with a black African that spends his days smoking weed, a South American looking for pussy in Lithuania, and all the other fuck-buddies he saw you with. "Not your type" means that you deserve much worse, the filthiest men available. Samantha said

I was calling her, because that's what she wished to see happening. She thinks she's better than you, and that you don't deserve a smart and mature man like me. That's why she used the "too old" argument against you. She thinks I should be looking for someone better, like her, because you are not good enough. And that's why she was fighting with Gintas so much, as she wanted freedom to find better than him. The worse thing for her is to see her dumb friend, i.e., you, with someone better than Gintas. Yes, Samantha is jealous of you. Because she wanted a guy that travels and has knowledge, and not a boring guy like Gintas. She cheated on Gintas and she will continue doing so, until she finds someone better. That's why she works for the Government — she's power driven, and a narcissist, and she doesn't have many friends just like you, because you both share the same mental disease. That's why she rather destroy your relationship than seeing you succeeding. And yet, by allowing her to do it, it's like you're kissing her ass. Going to her wedding, will be like kissing her ass publicly. And I wouldn't be surprised if she tries to humiliate you in her wedding just to entertain herself.

Naturally, she will always present you to single men she knows, as she has been doing this whole time since we are together, to make sure you date someone inferior but within her circle, to keep you from going anywhere in life. You are so dumb that you can't see that. And Ramune, she said that I am too ugly for you, because she, herself, has a very ugly man. She doesn't think that I'm ugly, but she said it because she wanted you to party with her and to be with someone worse, not a "serious man" as she said. Serious means mature, Gloria! She was not nervous near me because I'm serious, but because I made her feel stupid and childish. That's why she has fights with her ugly boyfriend. They fight because she is too stupid and childish, just like you are. Isn't ironic that she succeeds in destroying your relationship knowing that her relationship is much worse? But you don't dare telling her that her boyfriend is a hundred times uglier than anyone else, me included, right? But do you know what is the best for me? The best for me is to believe your friends, because you like them more than you ever liked me. If you always had fights with me since I met you because of them, if you agree with them on everything they say, and if you even fight to go meet them and trash me in the conversations you have with them, then the best for me is to really go with the flow as you do and believe what they say about you when talking about me. Because this is what they really say:

- Marius: "You deserve a woman that wants a family, not one who is a whore that likes to have sex with men she meets in clubs, and is always clubbing looking for new guys."

- Samantha: "You deserve a woman who is smart and wants to travel the world with you, and not idiot Gloria who doesn't even read and doesn't know anything about life."

- Ramune: "You should be with a woman who is serious and committed, and not one who is childish and irresponsible, and rather party than keeping her relationship intact."

If you put them first and ahead of me, it means they know you better than I do. The best for me is really to agree with them and find the type of woman they describe when triangulating you against me."

Gloria: — "You know, even if I don't go in Samantha's wedding, there is no way we will create a family. You are leaving anyway."

Adam: — "First, I was here for nearly three years and you even told me that you wanted to cheat on me for more than a year. After this confession, you went on partying for a whole month, most likely to fuck around too. Second, I don't trust you anymore, and you give me no reasons to trust you, because you are clearly a cheater, and I don't want to wait for that to happen in front of me."

Gloria: — "I am very nervous near you and I don't like myself when with you."

Adam: — "This is projection. What you really want to say is: 'I know that you, Adam, don't feel yourself near me.'"

Gloria: — "You never listen to me, you don't care."

Adam: — "Projection again: 'Me, Gloria, doesn't care about what you, Adam, have to say, and I don't listen to you.'"

Gloria: — "I don't want to share anything with you anymore."

Adam: — "You shared nothing that wasn't obvious already. The worse was what I had to find on my own — hundreds of messages you sent to men inviting them to your room. I have never seen anything so shocking in my entire life. But maybe you have no self-esteem yourself. I am ashamed of you. But maybe I have more respect for you than what you have for yourself or even for me."

Gloria: — "I am planning to rent an apartment on my own, you are leaving Lithuania. This is a relationship you want?"

Adam: — "No, this is the relationship you want. You never gave me the relationship I want. If I was able to control you, and manipulate you, as you say, I would have made you a better person and then married you, long time ago. But who is really controlling you and manipulating you? Your friends: Marius, Samantha and Ramune!"

Gloria: — "I cannot look at you anymore, I don't want to kiss you anymore. I feel forced."

Adam: — "People like you need to go downhill to learn. I know you want to find a guy better than me, but you won't find, because those guys don't like girls like you. You will always find guys for sex, but your relationships won't ever last more than ours."

Gloria: — "Even yesterday's sex was literally physical, because I felt nothing. You offended me so much that I feel no love anymore."

Adam: — "You never loved me. You said it yourself. So I don't know where this comes from."

Gloria: — "Everything makes me nervous; the way you live, your attire, your laugh, your jokes, your conversations, the way you walk. It's insane. I don't want that. I don't want that anymore..."

Adam: — "You have serious mental problems. It's not related to me."

Gloria: — "You should find a person who will love you honestly."

Adam: — "I agree. You never loved me and you were never honest. And this is probably the only truth you said so far."

Gloria: — "Interesting concept of relationship! I am saying that my opinion does not matter in this relationship, that you only say what you want and don't even bother yourself to listen to me and it's my fault again... You want just a doll, Adam, who does not talk. I want to have my voice and opinion, but I am not allowed that because, apparently, you have more knowledge. So I rather not talk with you at all, because it just doesn't make any sense. Only you matter."

Adam: — "You have no moral fiber, no ethics, no rules, no values, no nothing. That's why you can have sex with any stranger but feel nervous whenever there are emotions involved. You had sex with too many guys and you damaged yourself forever. Then you kept friendships that keep reinforcing your mental problems. And it's hard to deal with a person with serious mental problems, but worse than that is having to deal with a whole hospital of mental patients (your friends and family). I can tolerate and accept your family, because it is your family. But if you are not willing to cut off your friends from your life, like a cyst or cancer in your body, and if you cannot cut off alcohol and partying alone, I really have no interest in seeing you anymore.

If you really wanted to get married, you would. But you can't anymore, because you fucked so many guys, that now your concept of relationship is based on one night stands and the life of a single woman. You can't change from that past. And I know why, but I'm not your psychologist, and you became more evil to me because I tried to help you and "fix your head". You can change but for worse. Much worse! You basically used everything I did for you against me, by calling me suppressive, psychopathic and insane, which is what you are. One day you will be calling me narcissistic too. You already started saying to people that I beat you. But actually you started the violence multiple times and you deserved a beating more than once. You only respect violence, but then you twist the facts in your head, because of your childhood traumas.

I need a woman that knows how to appreciate me and respect me, and admire me. Love... you never loved me. You don't even know what love is. You are afraid to love. Every time you felt love in your heart, you slapped my balls, threw an umbrella at my face, or went on getting drunk with someone else to forget about it. You are damaged Gloria. The more I talk, the more you twist the words and use them against me. So there's no point for me anymore in being with you. You see Gloria, a person with mental problems and a traumatic childhood, like you, even if she turned out to be a whore, and fucked over thirty guys before 22yo, and is mentally damaged... I could still marry and take her out of Lithuania to travel with me wherever I go, to make me company and enjoy life by my side, as what you experienced in Portugal, Spain, France, Holland, Poland... But I need this woman to be a follower (not someone who betrays me by partying with people who try to end my relationship with her and even goes celebrate the wedding of such people), trustworthy (not someone who wants to party alone in England and go to Holland to see male strippers and couples having sex in public), and someone who respects what I say (not someone who insults every single thing I say). And you know what else Gloria, for three years, I have allowed you to damage my life, while I saw you enjoying yours. You are competing with me and you are revengeful, and much more. And that's the real problem here: You want a nice guy like me, but you hate nice guys. You don't have sex with nice guys. You only fuck with guys who look "cool", not nice. I made you lose interest in me because I was not as cool as you thought, but actually very serious and hard working, and you resented that."

Gloria: — "I want to socialize with people, and I felt way better when I met with my friends after our break up, but you don't understand it and you want me to be only with you. I am 25yo and you want to lock me in the house."

Adam: — "You were supposed to die not long ago, and it is because I came back to Lithuania that you did not. Whatsoever you did behind my back, attracted such a high level of bad karma towards you, that you had to go through that. And it should have been much harder than it was. But you do not know anything about the world you live in. You are spiritually blind. And I accept the fact that your soul has no chance anymore. I was your last chance, and I believe I did not met you by coincidence. You must have asked for something special before I appeared in your life. I just hope that you didn't pass me any sexually transmitted disease from the men you cheated on me with."

Gloria: — "If you think I passed you a disease, go and check."

Adam: — "If you had sex with someone else, or you sucked a stripper's cock in Holland, or fucked for fun "only once", or whatever you say to justify yourself, you should actually tell me, and not just send me to a doctor, to see if you can escape a confession. Because what you are saying, basically, is that you won't confess anything unless there is some prove. It's the same as always. And then you talk about creating a family, but you can't control yourself in front of other men, as I have seen myself and even heard from other people. And you blame me for wanting to be with you only for sex, even though you texted hundreds of men just because that is all you want. You even went clubbing with your friends because you like to seek for opportunities for sex, and you think it's not cheating when we're not together."

Gloria: — "I told you that I didn't slept with anybody, but you don't believe and blame me for the diseases you don't even have."

Adam: — "I need a woman who can help me achieve my goals in life. You are not that woman Gloria. You just want me stuck in Lithuania because your life is going nowhere. I have told you many times: I am first! Not

jealous-samantha, not retarded-Ramune, not cocksucker-Marius. We had many fights for nearly three years, for only one reason. Only one reason Gloria: You are stupid!

There was nothing wrong in obeying what I say. You are just too ignorant to see it. The problem begun when you started listening to what others say. Those others told you that it's cool to be a whore, get drunk, and smoke weed; those others told you that an independent woman parties alone and justifies nothing; those others told you that your life with me is boring and I want to control you; those others told you that you have the right to explore your opportunities and have sex with anyone. But I can't fight the whole world and still live my own life, or force you to see something that you can't see.

I know that you have been suffering a lot and struggling with your own thoughts, I also know that you often cry alone, but I already gave you three years of my life. If you wanted to learn, you would have learned already. Instead, you delayed my life, you insulted me multiple times, and you kept betraying my trust on you. But don't ask me to downgrade myself to the low level of the people you know. That is not love! That is the opposite of it! And most words coming out of your mouth, including the sarcastic, "You must be my guardian angel" came from the devil himself. Being sarcastic is not being smart, Gloria; sarcasm is the way the imbecile hide their ignorance about the world, when speaking in the tongue of demons.

I have loved a person named Gloria, but I only saw her once in a while, and I don't see her anymore. I don't know who you are. I don't see myself in your eyes, and I also don't see your own soul in your eyes. That is why I asked you if you like yourself. There's nothing strong about being evil, and there's nothing good in being self-destructive.

My life has always been good Gloria. Trying to prove me wrong, doesn't say anything about me. Says a lot about you only. You are not the same person I met, but worse. I don't recognize you anymore. You are like a demon full of anger and hate. Your lack of self-respect and lack of self-love is not my fault Gloria. And the psychologist you found, as your friends, used those two things against you. Yes, you are being manipulated all the time, by the people who tell you that you are "too pretty to make choices that they can't accept", "too smart to allow yourself to learn from a smarter person", "too young to grow up",... Your friends manipulate you very easily, by using your lack of self-respect and lack of self-love against you. And then you cry, for trusting them and destroying everything that you have in your life. But as I said, you haven't suffered enough yet, because I'm blocking your karma from coming in. You must have done really a lot of bad things to me, because your karma is very heavy, Gloria."

Confessions

Gloria tried to reconnect with me multiple times, but I wouldn't allow it, not without getting the answers I wanted and needed...

Adam: — "When you said to me in Poland, "If a guy loves a woman, it is ok that she cheats", you were again throwing another indirect confession of yours. Just as it was when you said that you planned to cheat for a whole year while living in my own house. Why did you even begged me to stay in Lithuania? Why did you begged me to let you join me in Poland? And you want to talk about loneliness? I became more alone when I met you, because wherever I take you, you want to flirt with any other man. You can't control yourself whenever you see a man. And I stopped going out because you seriously embarrass me in front of other people, and you make everyone I know feel embarrassed with your childish/whoring behavior. I basically lost my social life in Lithuania because of you. You know Gloria, when you cried like a baby and begged me not to leave Lithuania multiple times, and then told me that you planned to cheat on me for a whole year, and that this was the past and I should forget it, you have hit a very strong blow in my heart. And after that, you went to party with your friends every night, all night, to have sex with other guys. That is cruel beyond belief. When I returned, you ended up in hospital, and I went to visit you every day and even cooked for you and stopped my work entirely during that period. Then, in return, you repeated the exact same behaviors. You gave me the same insults, and you then went on partying with people who insult me, like Samantha. How can you be so ungrateful and disgusting with someone who does so much for you? And now you want to tell me that I'm the crazy one, and that you are not interested in me anymore? Am I a joke to you?

ROWAN KNIGHT

When I met you, you asked me if I would dump you if everyone I know did not like you. Now I see why. You also asked me why I dumped other women. Now I see why. You also said that you can't control yourself and you are an idiot with all men. Now I see why. There is really nothing to do anymore for someone who can't even learn from either her past experiences, or a near death experience. Your life was going downhill before you met me, and it is still going downhill now. But at least you had many chances to change it. You should have ditched your friends, cut the communication with your past, to realize how much you could get, like a winning lottery ticket fallen from the sky. Your dear friends made you and it is really sad that you can't see that you have been fooled by other people, and allowed yourself to destroy your own health — mental and physical, as well as your future. You are only a victim of yourself. You created what you have. And if you think you can find better than me, I wish you good luck, because the last thing I ever wanted was a woman that disrespects me and stops me from living the life of my dreams, which, ironically, is the same life you wanted for yourself. Every single conversation with you, goes around in the same circles: "I did not get drunk; And if I did, was long time ago; And if I got drunk, that's not a big deal; And if it is, is not my fault — they put the drinks in front of me; And if I got drunk, I didn't want to; And if I wanted to get drunk, it's your fault you were in Ukraine." Or "I did not fuck a bunch of guys; And if I did, everyone does it anyway; And if I fucked lots of guys, I did not got paid like a prostitute; And if I behaved like a prostitute, it's because I need sex; And if I was a whore, is because I was single; And if I can't unfuck them, that's your problem."

What would you tell me one day about cheating? I did not cheat; And if I did, was only once; And if I cheated, that's the past now, and you should shut up; And if I cheated, it's not my fault — someone else put his dick in front of me; And I I fucked another guy, I didn't mean it; And if I did mean it, you deserved it?

What was even the point of making yourself hard to get for me, if any other guy can snap his fingers and your legs open automatically? You like to make good people look stupid, because you are an ungrateful person? I did for you what no other man did, but you were not worth even one night of sex. Next time you envy other women and their relationships, remember nobody wants a dying alcoholic whore with psychiatric problems like you anyway. And may

DESTINY: WHEN YOUR SOULMATE FINDS YOU

God have mercy on your soul, because it drifts in Hell. You never appreciated me, who I really am, or everything I did for you. Why should any man want you? A slut, cheater, liar, with mental problems, and a high probability of getting cancer, always insulting, always manipulating, always flirting with other men with no shame,... and you even admit it: "I like when men look at me like they want to fuck me." You were doing that with me next to you, and a gold engagement ring in your finger. And then you complained to me that we never go out and have no friends. Where can I go with an idiot like you? What kind of wife do you think you can become? I don't know what you wanted from me this whole time, but nothing good in my life happened from meeting you. You transformed my entire life, not just into a circus, but a whole psychiatric hospital."

Gloria: — "You opinion about me is formed from the things I did when you didn't even know me."

Adam: — "The things you did before I met you, make you who you are — a whore and a disgusting slut. What changed after you met me? You flirted in front of me multiple times, continued to try and see if you have chances with new men, and you even said to me: "You are too ugly for me, and I tried to cheat on you because I deserve better".

Do you think I forget that or the condoms in your purse or the nights out not telling me where you go? The problem is not in me Gloria but in you, and it is not in the past but in the present, and in the person you really are, not the person you pretend to be — you are not a woman but a child, you are only committed to your own fun and to having the attention of different men, you do not know what it is to be with one man only — committed in a monogamous relationship.

What went wrong? I thought I could change you. That is what went wrong. I'm fed up of your constant lies and your constant attempts at making me look like I am the crazy one because you cannot admit you are a horrible person. What did you bring to my life Gloria? Misery, suffering and craziness? You don't miss me. You just want a toy to play with. Go get a puzzle or a lego. You are a child. Not a woman! And being a whore didn't make you a woman. Made you a whore with an infantile brain. That's who you are behind the mask you show other people."

Gloria: — "My puzzle is in your house."

Adam: — "You know how to talk to a boy you want to fuck for one night. You don't know how to talk to a man you insulted and disrespected in multiple ways for years. I'm perfectly fine with being fat and ugly and not your type, or being hated by your friends and brother. I have disconnected from all that while detaching from the source — you. Everything that came through you to my life was negative. I need a woman and you'll never be that. You will just be a 25yo child and a 35yo child and a 40yo child.

I rented an expensive house because of you, stayed for nearly three years in Lithuania because of you, and this whole time you were hooking with other guys and partying with the rats of your friends. What do you know about love? When I met you, you were going to hotel rooms with a bunch of guys, hoping to get gang banged in a major fuck fest. Then, when you were with me, you were chatting and meeting with ex-boyfriends. What do you want more?

Look, Gloria, I don't want to marry you anymore. I have given up on that delusional idea long time ago. You are not the wife I want. I don't want to have babies with you. You're totally incompetent to be a mother. An alcoholic, cheating, weed smoking mother? Give me a break! How many times have you cheated that you hide? Because I have seen how you lie. You lie so well, that a person needs to be totally insane to lie as you do. And isn't your brother against me? Isn't your mother telling you to quit the relationship? Isn't Viktorija saying that I'm too old for you? Isn't your sister telling you that nothing is your fault and the relationship just doesn't work? Aren't your coworkers telling you that career comes first and men are losers that need a woman wearing pants at home? Didn't your beloved psychologist told you that I manipulate you? How can someone even take so much? I don't want to live the rest of my life with a whore that fucks half the world and dumps the garbage of other people on me. You make me sick and ashamed. That's how I feel whenever I am with you in front of others, because I know I am living a lie with a fake person. I will never be proud of you."

Gloria: — "Understood! I will take my last things and won't bother you anymore ever again."

Adam: — "When I met you, you were hitting on all men, and ignoring me all the time. You even went with Arthuro and his friends to a hotel room where you slept the night, just to get sex. You never agreed to meet me, but you were taking rides from Tomas, going out on dates with Arthuro, and so on. I asked you a simple question when we went out for the first time, and you said "no", regarding one night stands. And then I find that you are prostituting yourself in your room, sleeping with a naked man every night... to which you replied "I do whatever I want when I'm single" and "it's not prostitution when I don't get money, and just fuck voluntarily"... Jesus Christ, those are the most disturbing and sick and disgusting words I ever heard in my entire life.

You moved in to my house, asked for a ring, and kept cheating on me, flirting with men in front of me, because you "like the look in their eyes when they want to fuck", but you couldn't find anyone you like, or that liked you, otherwise, as you said, "you would dump me". And now you love me? Did you realize it after having sex with another guy while I was in Ukraine? Is that why you asked me why I came back so many times? I even caught you looking at another guy last time, in Kaunas. Some things just never change. You are who you are! I cannot teach you moral, ethics and compassion. Some people just don't have it. You don't have it. You are a very sick evil being. Not a woman! I wish our fights had anything to do with you being a woman. They don't. They're not about that. All the fights are about me expecting a psychopathic being without emotions to understand the consequences of her actions, from the past and present. It won't ever happen. It would be a breakthrough in psychology if I ever made it happen. You don't love me Gloria. You are a liar. I'm certain, that as soon as I'm gone, you'll start sleeping with someone else, even in the same day, if possible.

Maybe I expected too much from you, but I don't believe we are meant to stay together. You have your path to experience. And it was a mistake to see you before you ended in that hospital. It should have been someone else. I did that mistake too. But the biggest mistake, the greatest mistake of all, was to believe you could be fixed when I met you. You are broken. At 22yo, you were already completely broken. Things won't ever get better from now. But there are many losers in this world that will accept you after one night stand. And you know that. You have the confidence of a slut. And I will never be able to make friends for as long as you are in my life. Besides, if you had to choose between getting drunk, and taking care of a child, you would choose getting drunk. If you think I "make you nervous", how much more nervous would you get with a child or two? Like my crazy mother, I bet. Nobody makes you nervous Gloria. You are simply the result of a psychopathic brain mixed with weed and alcohol abuse.

And how ironic is life, when the only person who knows everything about you and how to fix you, is the only person you don't trust, and the one you hate and insult the most. The truth hurts because you are insane. All that prostitution, weed, alcohol, and evilness, comes with a price. And I do believe the God you don't believe in, sent me to your life to have a second chance. Because your own hatred against me has speed up your karma. And it's awful horrible to see a person paying back for what she does.

Do you know why I asked you to stop getting drunk and smoking weed, and why I cared so much about how many guys you had sex with? Because, Gloria, that's a turning point in your life. You are too deep within hell. I can't pull you back anymore. I have to move on."

Gloria: — "You said everything you wanted. I wish happiness for you. I just cannot believe you were smiling in my face, making love, hugging, kissing, being nice. I feel so sad and upset. I am missing you so much. But you are right. We are not supposed to be together. Indeed, I will not go anywhere in my life, because I am diving in the darkness. For me the strangest thing is that you know the most about how the brain works, emotions, suppressions and etc, but you spit directly in my face all the things with no remorse and I put this in my head and devalue myself. I don't blame you for anything. I need you, but you don't need me. There was no relationship between us. Every week splitting apart... I am becoming jealous of any crapy relationship because I don't have any at all. I cannot even relax, cannot not think, not cry, I hide my emotions, and I'm tired of not having a person to talk to. I cannot handle this anymore."

Adam: — "I am not your father or mother. They failed in raising you and it's not my responsibility to fix you. You are old enough to do that for yourself. If you have chosen to waste your life by having sex with strangers, smoking weed and getting drunk every weekend, that is your problem. Because, you see, when I was 23yo, I was already working very hard on myself, and spending lots of money on books and courses to help myself, to fix myself. At your age, I was already in many religions and even seeing a psychologist. I was not wasting myself and my time and waiting for a woman to save me. You save yourself, Gloria. I have taken too much pain from you. I have no more patience for your insults and provocations. I am not responsible for your life. You have chosen to destroy the relationship. That is your problem; not mine. I have a life to live. You are ruining it. Even your voice irritates me now. Your presence, happy or mad, annoys me. I have no desire to be with you anymore. I felt pity but pity was replaced by disgust and sickness. To trust you was like swimming with sharks hoping not to die. I do like you, but we have reached a point in which I realize it will never work. There is too much anger in you which you target at me. You do hate many people in your life, but you suppress it, and then you release that anger against me and only me. And that, from what I see, will never end. You have gained the habit of attacking me because it is easy for you. You feel safe with me but you also feel safe to attack me. And such attacks made you disrespect me even more. I do not see myself in your eyes anymore. And If you hate the person you think you love then you are not in love with that person. You are in love with your own hate. I do love you but your hate sets me apart. You want a lot from life but you are not at the level of the things you want. You want to get married but you don't behave like a wife, or even a girlfriend. Far from that! You behave like a potential cheater and a dishonest woman. I don't want to live with a person that takes pleasure in hurting me and suppressing me all the time. And I certainly cannot be in a relationship with someone that is selfish, only thinks about her own wants and desires, and ignores my needs entirely. I need someone that is more mature, respectful and friendly. Your level of responsibility and commitment is so very low, that you even laugh at my face whenever I catch you doing something offensive. You take pride in hurting me with cheating behaviors and I really despise people that do that. I cannot imagine myself living with such a person and face such situations for the rest of my life. Your words do not mean anything, when you apologize, cry and regret, because you keep doing the same. And there is a pleasure in hurting me that you have learned to enjoy, like a tiger that has tasted blood for the first time. And that, Gloria, is called Emotional Vampirism. You like to hurt and I can't accept that.

I feel sad to see that such a young person is so damaged already. I am very sorry for you. But I do not want to be hurt anymore. And I don't think you can have a healthy relationship with me. Your purpose this whole time has been to prove me wrong, and not to look in the mirror and see yourself for who you really are.

I wrongly believed that because you are still young, you would not be as damaged as many people I met before. I also wrongly believed that you are shy, friendly and naive. I had no idea of the many one night stands you had, your predatory pursue of foreign men for sex, and your super aggressive nature in relationships. I also thought that your aggressive nature was just superficial. I had no idea you would hurt me more than anyone else and use me to funnel all the anger you have towards other people. I have dealt with many angry people in my life but I do not want that anymore. I have also dealt with manipulative and dishonest people, but I do not want that anymore either. I do appreciate your efforts to change, but I have not seen the changes I was expecting. You make me feel embarrassed with your behavior, either in public or in private, and you use what you learn from me to become better at manipulating me and provoking me. You did not use any of the knowledge to behave better. And this shows that you have chosen not to get better. You have chosen to hurt me instead. Knowledge will just make you stronger in that path and purpose.

You broke my trust on you, piece by piece, until none was left. And I told you this, but you seemed determined to destroy the relationship from the start. It was as if the more information I handed you, the more you would use it against me. You do not respect me or what I do, and you do not respect my past and what I suffered living with women like you. I do not love you enough to accept so much anger. I tried but it's more than I can handle. And I don't deserve that anger directed at me. I didn't do anything to you to deserve so much hate. And I do not want to be with someone that is constantly planning revenge against me, as if I had no right to tell you to stop. You are an abusive person, and I hope one day you can find the light you lost, in therapy, religion or within your own self. I wish for you that one day you can let go of that darkness inside of you that you learned to accept and call home. I hope that one day you can shutdown the voice in your head, talking to you from a realm that is strange to your soul. And I hope one day you can stop being afraid of people like me. I did not enter your life to hurt you or to be hurt. It is not my fault that the relationship did not work. I did my best to make you happy. Your arrogance, selfishness and evilness are not compatible with your stupidity, laziness and psychopathic lack of empathy for me. The only emotions you know are fear and anger, because you are mentally sick, trapped inside childhood traumas.

I gave you an engagement ring for what? Didn't you chat with Andreas and flirted with other guys in the street after getting that ring? You deserve nothing. And you dare to ask me for another ring? If you did not love me before, and for so long, then you used me for sex, right? So why do you get offended when

I tell you that I can have sex with you without feelings? If offends you when another person is like you? Your existence offends you, right? When I tell you what you tell me, it offends you and hurts you, right? But you still insult me in the same way, after I showed you that, because you are a hypocrite. You should stop spending your time with losers, following what losers do and wasting your time with nonsense, and increase the value of your life by doing things that increase your self-esteem and your personal value as a human being."

Gloria: — "I want to be with you, Adam. I am hurt, I feel angry, mad, sad and disappointed. But at the same time I miss you, I want to walk with you, talk to you, just be with you, be next to you and be with you."

Adam: — "I don't know the future but I never wanted a woman that is selfish and dependent on other people's for validation, especially men. If you want to be someone's wife one day, learning to be submissive to the person of your choice is a good start. I would never accept a woman with bitchy attitude. That's why things didn't work. You just have to look back to see what happened. But don't demand things from me, because at this point I am very confused Gloria. You hurt me a lot and you confused me in many ways. Many things that I found about you shocked me, because you were only 22yo when I met you. I don't want to fight anymore, but you need to think about your behaviors when you are alone."

The Painful Truth

The agreements wouldn't last long, as usual. Gloria would meet me days later, with another attempt at destroying our relationship...

Gloria: — "I am going on Samantha's Wedding."

Adam: — "Samantha is humiliating you and you don't even see it. She wants you to go on her weeding after lying about me, telling you that I wanted to cheat on you with her, because she wants to destroy your life. Going to her wedding is like putting her above you."

Gloria: — "If she humiliates me, not you, why do you care? You are 38yo and you play these games."

Adam: — "The fact that you are going on her wedding proves that you are extremely mentally sick, much more than I thought. This time you won't get to see me anymore or even get replies. If your purpose in talking to her is to push me away, consider it a victory. Enjoy the celebration of your imbecility! I have nothing more to tell you. You have been a very disappointing person in my life."

Gloria: — "Whatever!"

Adam: — "Everything about you is too degrading to watch. You sleep with a gay, you text random guys for sex, you go on a wedding alone of a person who destroys your relationship due to jealousy... after partying with Ramune who did the same. You are so degrading Gloria,... so low in mental health.... So disgusting,... that knowing you was the most sickening experience of my life."

Gloria: — "Again and again and again and again..."

Adam: — "You have been brutalizing the relationship since day one. Just stay alone. Do a favor to this world who already has too much suffering and don't even date anyone, or better yet, go destroy evil people like you and have relationships with them before committing suicide or getting killed with AIDS. And consider it a miracle you were in my life because you have no value whatsoever as a human being. If you cannot quit going to Samantha's wedding and insist on it, and if you insist on judging me, I really don't feel like seeing you for the rest of my life. I know what you are doing. You enjoy being evil. It's just too sick to have you in my life."

Gloria: — "I did a lot for you already and didn't work. It will never work. I will just keep on losing people because of you and we will breakup anyway. This was already like this for almost three years. It is too long. At least I could keep you company before you leave."

Adam: — "What did you actually do? It will never work with anyone. And you are losing people? Who is people? Samantha is people? Yes, it was too long for me, not for you. I was the one wasting my life. Nothing changed in your life. I am the one who was always happy and now is always angry. I don't even want your company anymore. I don't want to think of you, text you or see you anymore."

Days after this argument, I still tried to give a last opportunity to the relationship, but Gloria was already with someone else when I texted her, and decided to avoid me on this Sunday night. She couldn't wait for the relationship to end, and immediately jumped into a new relationship in less than ten days. However, she hided it from me, to keep me in the dark about it, possibly as a backup plan in case it didn't work.

Adam: — "We need to talk before I leave."

Gloria: — "Today I cannot. I am going in an excursion about a Lithuanian painter. I can meet you tomorrow even before work."

Adam: — "You are going in an excursion with who? Why do you lie? We can meet before your date. Takes about 30min and you are coming in the center anyway. You can then spend the night having sex with your new boyfriend. I just want to talk for 30min or less. I know you have someone new. I'm letting you go. I just want to talk something important and then you can go back to your life with him."

Gloria: — "I am going in the excursion at 10PM. It will finish at 11PM. I can meet you after. I am going with Samanta."

Adam: — "Great! You can meet me around 9PM, or I can find you and Samantha later. Which you prefer?"

Gloria: — "I am at her place now. I cannot meet you today. I can meet you tomorrow."

Adam: — "So many lies. I'm going in the center. Where can I find you? Answer!"

Gloria: — "What the hell, I was having a conversation. The world doesn't go around you."

Adam: — "Where and at what time I find you today? Answer me!"

Gloria: — "I cannot meet you today. Only tomorrow! What do you want to say? I am not playing anything, Adam. Can be a time for us tomorrow at any time. For your own comfort I can pass by any place where you are"

Adam: — "At what time?"

Gloria: — "What do you want to say that you cannot say here? I will meet you tomorrow at 6PM."

Adam: — "Are you in the center right now?"

Gloria: — "Yes."

Adam: — "So I meet you in the center."

Gloria: — "No, not today. I will not meet you today. Tomorrow at 5PM."

Adam: — "Finish earlier to meet me. Deal?"

Gloria: — "I cannot finish earlier. What are you taking?"

Adam: — "I don't think his name is Samantha. Where are you? Can't you even wait before you start sleeping with someone else? You lie too much. It's too messed up to schedule meeting me tomorrow after sleeping with someone else today. You take your insanity too far Gloria. You don't want to be caught cheating but I only want to talk to you. Can't you tell the new guy to wait 15min before you open your legs?"

Gloria: — "You are talking nonsense. I am with her and we are going home. I see you tomorrow."

Adam: — "It's the same thing for three years. There's always a "Samantha". Have fun with "Samantha"."

Gloria: — "Believe what you want. If I was with a guy, I wouldn't even chat with you."

Adam: — "There's no need to lie anymore Gloria. You're not sleeping in your place and you're not a teenager anymore, and that's all I need to know. Enjoy the night."

Gloria: — "Yes, I am sleeping at Samanta's place."

In the following day...

Adam: — "You agreed yesterday to meet, so I appreciate you don't waste my time with more of your lies. If you said you will meet me today after getting fucked last night, then you will. Then you can keep going to be a whore forever. Deal? I just want to talk."

Gloria: — "So I can meet you at 4PM."

I met with Gloria, but not to talk to her anymore as there was no point. She was different. She couldn't even look at my eyes. She was clearly having sex with someone else already. Her whole behavior showed me that she had spent the weekend sleeping with another man. And she had bags of clothes in her hands proving it. She must have felt ashamed of herself because she tried to avoid me, saying she had to go somewhere else and had no time to talk with me. I was also already prepared for this. So when I realized that there were fewer people around, I stepped in front of her, as if to kiss her, and she disarmed, and relaxed her shoulders. At that moment I took her hand and stole her cell phone. I insisted that she should tell me the password or I would throw the phone in the river nearby, but she refused and started yelling, as if I was a common thief...

— "Give me the cell phone!"

She wanted to draw the attention of people passing by to interfere, but I was ready for this as well. That morning, I went to the hairdresser, cut my hair, and was wearing nice shoes and an expensive shirt, like a businessman. So when people looked at me, they did not realize it was a robbery. It actually was. I never did this before, but my patience was over. As she kept yelling and refused to cooperate, I started running with her cell phone in my pocket. She came after me but could not catch me. When I arrived home, I hid her cell phone. She rang the bell and I opened the door, but asked for the wallet with the money, and said I would give it back if she cooperated. At that point, she stopped screaming and acting violent as usual. I placed her wallet on the porch and asked her to put the password on the cell phone. She then sat in front of me while I was erasing everything — all the videos and photos that we took together for three years. Everything! I would make sure that she did not have any more memories of us. And I saw a lot that I wasn't prepared to see. She had many photos of me completely naked in bed or making a foolish face. No wonder she saw me as the idiot she had sex with — that was all she wanted to photograph to remember. It's like living with a photographer always waiting for your worst moments, even as you sleep, or get distracted, even your mocking faces, to catch the worst of you, and then portray you like some cartoon character without a personality.

I then returned the cell phone and wallet and put her out of the house, telling her,...

— "Looking at the photos in your mobile made me feel sick, angry and sad at the same time. Because it is as if my life was an invention without meaning. I am not the person who appears in the photos, but the version you wanted me to be — a pathetic fool to entertain you like a monkey. It is a traumatic experience to see reality through the eyes of a person like you. My mistake was to think that I could help you not be evil anymore; I offered you my house, and it did not work; I was the only person visiting you in the hospital when you nearly died and bringing you cooked food every day, and you did not care either; I never disrespected you to your family or lied about you to them as you did to me, and you did not care either; I was patient with you and your evilness, and you did not care either; I took you to travel with me to several countries and you did not appreciate either... In the end, you used me to set me up, provoking me to create videos with my reactions, and destroy my reputation. That is beyond evil,... it is psychopathic... it is very sick. I would never do such things to you. And I had many chances, of just filming you acting insane, as always, but I never even thought about doing it. And from the photos taken, I can see that you had a very good life with me... you just can't be happy. And that's the real problem here; You can't be happy. But God always answers my prayers, and I prayed a lot for a resolution. I really did. And you don't believe in God but you will know that He is real, because He will keep distracting you, with people that appear out of nowhere to remove you from my life. You will keep meeting many other men after me, and when months later it all collapses, you will remember me, and you will know that God is real, because I do not wish and I never wished anything bad to happen to you, but karma will come rushing in at a faster speed once I am out of your life. I just don't even want to see your face anymore. I don't even want sex with you anymore. You disgust me. You are so sick that having sex with you disgusts me profoundly. Don't even text me sex offers anymore. Don't even ask me for a 69."

Gloria: — "69 is just a number."

Adam: — "Not when you reach that age and you are completely alone. Then you will know it's not just a number."

Gloria: — "I'm sorry! It was my fault to talk to you like this."

Adam: — "Just leave!"

Gloria: — "Thank you for what you did for me, Adam."

Adam: — "I know who you are now. I know how disgusting and evil you truly are. I know how worthless and vindictive you are. I have seen the world through your eyes and found how insane is your nature. All your relationships will fail and you will forever pay for cheating on me and all the lies you told me. You will never be happy. You will always be miserable. But that I already know for a long time. The difference Gloria is that I stoped caring. You crossed the boundaries too many times and you tried to destroy the only person who ever truly helped you. You will keep on having sex with other guys that Samantha and other friends will present you and you will forever celebrate your imbecility. And your mental disease will literally destroy you. And I pity you because of all the diseases you will get during your life. But I will not watch your misery again. You are like a vampire inside your own horror movie. It was interesting to watch you from 22 to 25yo, but my role in your movie has come to an end. I pity your misery. I pity your tears. But you are too evil and insane to deserve compassion. The irony of your story is that in your entire existence on this planet you will never find anyone capable of helping you. I was the only one. You used my help against me and lost it for doing that. You are too stupid to know what you lost and keep loosing. Your life came to an end when I ended with you. Do not try to come back to me after your many future failures. I don't even want you to think of me. I want you as far as possible."

Gloria: — "I appreciate what you gave me."

Adam: — "I'm sure you appreciated a lot when fucking with others. Tell your bullshit to those who are mentally retarded enough to care! What you did to me will never be forgotten. Keep on being the filthy whore you were before you met me. That's who you really are! You once told me: "Who do you think you are? My Guardian Angel?" And to that I answer you: Thank you! This is a perfect ending to our story. Isn't it amazing how, by predicting the future, I saved your life, for you to repeat it all over again? Except that this time, it's over. I will never come back."

The Revelation

It thought that everything had ended between us, and I started packing and selling my stuff, in order to move out of the house, and to another country. But weeks later Gloria tried to find me again. Either her new relationship wasn't working or she simply missed me.

Gloria: — "Can I invite you for a coffee? Without any bad intention."

Adam: — "I am reading a book in a coffee shop in the old town. You can meet me here."

When she arrived, Gloria was wearing a miniskirt and acted very politely and carefully to avoid making me angry in any way. Her voice was smooth and gentle too.

Gloria: — "Hi, How you are you? What have you been doing lately?"

Adam: — "Did you come to say goodbye?"

Gloria: — "Not necessarily, unless that's what you want."

Adam: — "I did so much for you and you were always trying to provoke me to make videos. Why?"

Gloria: — "Because if you beat me, I have evidence to show to the police."

Adam: — "So you were basically trying to put me in jail for no reason."

Gloria became quiet.

Adam: — "Did you have sex with anyone else lately?"

Gloria: — "No, but I kissed a guy on Samantha's weeding", Gloria said proudly.

Adam: — "How many times have you cheated on me or was that the only time?"

Gloria: — "It was only this time. I am telling you the truth. But we were not together anymore so it's not cheating."

Adam: — "Why did you do it?"

Gloria: — "The guy was very attractive and I wanted to kiss him."

Adam: — "I tolerated you for three years because of your tears... I spent entire days in the hospital with you, after you partied for a month like a drunk stupid whore with your friends... you had tubes coming out of your body and you were receiving a blood transfusion... you were a total mess... and I didn't abandon you... Even if you may die one day from ovarian cancer and never give birth to a child of mine, I never let you go, and you kiss some random guy in a party? What kind of a disgraceful human being are you?"

Gloria: — "I cannot be thankful to you all my life just because you helped me."

Adam: — "And I bet you kissed the guy in front of Samantha didn't you?"

Gloria: — "Yes! Actually, I kissed him in front of everyone. Everyone saw."

Adam: — "You literally kissed Samantha in the ass after she tried to destroy your relationship, as if performing a degrading show for her. That's so humiliating!"

Gloria: — "What are you talking about?"

Adam: — "How can you be so empty? Is there nothing inside of you?"

Gloria: — "We weren't together. We broke up. Let's go for a walk near the river and talk about something else."

I agreed but was still in shock. On the way, I stepped forward, in front of her, touched her with my left hand in her right shoulder, and asked once more...

—"Did you really kiss another guy?"

— "We were not even together anymore", she answered with arrogance and a proud smile to match it. And that's when my right hand flew against her face at high speed, and as hard as I could hit.

— "No, Gloria! Now, we are not together, for sure."

She took her left hand to the face, surprised, and said nothing. And I turned my back on her and left.

From the distance, I watched her walk back home, as if it was just another normal day. She didn't cry, didn't stop to think about what she did for a second, didn't apologize, didn't respond with not even one word. Before catching the bus, I saw her texting to someone, most likely telling her new boyfriend that everything between me and her was over for good. Yes, we had ended. But we were also soulmates meant to find each other. I was cleaning her karma too. And now her fate would go in another direction, the same path that

DESTINY: WHEN YOUR SOULMATE FINDS YOU

I interrupted by entering her life. It was in our destiny to meet and fall in love and build a family together, travel the whole world and enjoy life to the fullest. It was our shared dream, to have a beautiful relationship while exploring the entire planet hand in hand. And many miracles would have occurred if Gloria had remained with me. She would have never ended in that hospital, she would have never cheated with anyone, and she would certainly have a baby with me, even if a miracle was necessary for that to happen. But Gloria changed this destiny, a destiny that could only manifest through two soulmates. After that day, Gloria's life went on a complete and quick downward karmic spiral. Her closest friends, who had been telling her to abandon me, abandoned her, after insulting her and humiliating her in public several times, just as she had done with me for three years. Her experience with the new job became unbearable, as people bullied her, invalidated her and discriminated her inside the office, exactly as she had done with me at home, especially, after noticing how manipulative, narcissistic and selfish she is. Gloria eventually got fired when least expecting it, and felt abandoned just as she abandoned me, ending up with nothing, just as she did to me. She found herself without opportunities for new jobs and without friends. Counting on her savings only, she moved to her parent's house in the country side, where she would experience what she made me experience for three years — loneliness.

During the many endless days of depression and despair, Gloria realized what she had lost, and cried for hours in bed. This loss could only be forgotten during brief moments of the morning by the sun's rays emerging from between the trees of the forest. She remembered, while observing the sunshine from the window of her room, how I loved the morning and told her that waking up looking at her eyes was the best moment of my day. She still had these memories to hold on to, as if it was the only thing left in her life. Because never again would Gloria gain another opportunity to be cured and experience true love. And indeed, only love could cure her from a tendency to grow cysts in her body and cancer too. She spent her afternoons walking in the forest, listening to the birds, and trying to gain back her joy for life, just as I taught her. Her need to develop relationships based on physical attraction and validation, rather than love, made her emptier as a human being. After that last day with me, Gloria never again had a relationship that would last so long, and never again did she found a man that could make her feel the way she felt with me.

With every man she slept with, she remembered me, and with those memories came the unbearable flashbacks of her mistakes. But she couldn't handle the guilt or the fact that, by now, I was already married to someone else, younger and more attractive than she was. She couldn't deal with the fact that I had moved forward, formed my own family, and got everything that she wasn't able to provide me — a healthy marriage with a beautiful wife, well-educated, handsome and healthy children, and a luxurious lifestyle exploring the many countries of the world.

Gloria did stalk me on social media for a very long time, because she couldn't let go of her past with me, and with every photo of my family, my beautiful wife and our amazing children, it was as if she was cutting herself deeply in the chest with the regret of what she had done to herself. The emotional pain was unbearable, and she tried to commit suicide several times without success. She couldn't handle that tremendous contradiction, that I was having a fulfilling life, becoming wealthier and wealthier every day, that I was happier, and that I was more popular than ever before, while she was living miserably, sad and alone, with nothing to validate her existence. The only thing Gloria could get were empty relationships with men that used her for sex only, as she falsely accused me of doing to her. Because of that, she grew bitter, resentful, and remorseful. Her hatred once directed at me, reverted now back at her, and became very evident in her appearance.

Gloria felt relieved when years later she was diagnosed with terminal cancer. She wanted to die anyway. When the doctor gave her the news, she reacted as always, without any fear, any remorse, any sympathy for herself. She did not even cry. She accepted her fate as if she didn't care about her existence any longer, and was happy to finally end it.

I did fulfill my destiny, meant to be shared with Gloria, but with another woman. After Gloria died during the night, alone in the hospital, she was able to witness this happiness, and feel it with tears, as the ghost of a woman who had perished with a deadly diseased that could have been cured with true love — the spiritual love of a soulmate.

Book Review Request

Dear Reader, Thank you for purchasing this book! I would love to know your opinion. Writing a book review helps in understanding readers and also has an impact on other reader's purchasing decisions. Your opinion matters. Please write a book review! Your kindness is greatly appreciated!

Booklist

Books written by the author:

Agne: Inside the Mind of a Narcissist
Destiny: When Your Soulmate Finds You
Disenchanted: Poems by Rowan Knight
Illusion: When a Nymphomaniac Falls in Love
One Chance: 20 Short Stories with a Plot Twist and Moral Lesson
Prophecy: A Message to Humanity
Slave: Fulfilling a Prophecy
Soulless: Letters to a Narcissist

About the Publisher

This book was published by the 22 Lions Bookstore.
For more books like this visit www.22Lions.com.
Join us on social media at:
Fb.com/22Lions;
Twitter.com/22lionsbookshop;
Instagram.com/22lionsbookshop;
Pinterest.com/22LionsBookshop.